THE MEMORY BETWEEN TWO PAGES

VIGNESH AYYATHURAI

To my Grandmother, your love is my quiet strength.
And to the beautiful souls of my college, whose warmth and stories shaped

this journey, this is for you.

Contents

Acknowledgements

Writing this book has been a journey filled with learning, reflection, and gratitude.

First and foremost, I thank my family for their unwavering support, patience, and quiet encouragement, your belief in me made this possible. To the mentors and colleagues who sparked my curiosity and challenged me to see buildings beyond bricks and walls, thank you for inspiring deeper thought.

To every reader who picks up this book, thank you for taking the time to walk through these pages with me. I hope it brings insight, comfort, or simply a new way of seeing things.

This may be my first book, but it was never a solo journey. I'm deeply grateful to everyone who has been part of it.

CHAPTER ONE

THE TRAIN TO A NEW WORLD

The sky was the color of lullabies; a pale lavender stretch of soft nothing, gently giving way to gold. The sun hadn't fully risen, but its presence pressed lightly against the edge of the ocean, like a secret being whispered from far away. The waves, too, were hesitant, lapping against the shore in slow motion, as if unsure whether to wake the world or let it sleep a little longer.

Vihaan stood barefoot on the narrow porch where the old cement met the warm sand. The red towel, his towel hung lopsided from the coiled wire above him, still damp from yesterday's swim. It fluttered like a reluctant flag, refusing to admit that something was ending. He had not packed it. Couldn't. That towel had seen him through everything sea salt in his wounds, stolen naps in the sun, monsoon storms that sent shivers up his spine. It had dried his skin, his tears, and once, even a mango he dropped in the sand. Folding it into a suitcase felt like folding away a piece of himself.

Behind him, the house stirred in whispers. The creak of ceiling wood, the soft rustle of his mother's cotton saree as she moved between rooms. The clink of steel tumblers meeting the sink, the sharp hiss of mustard seeds hitting ghee in a hot kadai. The smell of roasted coconut drifted through the windows, colliding with the sea breeze a scent so layered, it could only belong to this house.

To this morning

To this moment.

Aachi was awake. Vihaan could hear the soft chant of Sanskrit verses coming from the puja room, not loud, not pleading, but steady, like the tide. It was always like this. God got the first hello.

Vihaan looked out toward the ocean. The horizon was a painting that hadn't dried yet. Somewhere out there, beyond the mist and gull cries, was Mumbai. A city of glass and pace. A place that didn't know his name. Yet.

But here, in this moment, he was still Vihaan from the beach barefoot, thoughtful, and aching in a way he didn't fully understand.

He bent down and picked up a smooth pebble from the sand. Cool to the touch, oval like a dropped almond. He rolled it in his palm for a moment, then slipped it into his pocket.

A souvenir for the parts of him that might forget.

The screen door gave its signature groan not quite a protest, not quite a greeting. Vihaan didn't need to turn around to know who it was.

"Kanna," his mother called softly, her voice careful not to wake the moment too loudly. "Come eat something before it gets cold."

Vihaan turned. She stood there in the doorway, framed by the fading blue of the old doorframe, one hand balancing a steel plate, the other holding a neatly folded towel. Her hair was freshly washed and twisted into a bun that looked like a jasmine bud waiting to bloom. Her saree, tucked up just slightly to avoid the sand, had a pattern of turmericcolored sunbursts the same one she wore every time someone left the house for something big. An exam. A job interview. A funeral. She had never called it lucky, but it always found its way onto her that morning.

She stepped down onto the porch, her anklets barely making a sound. With the tenderness only a mother could possess, she adjusted the collar of Vihaan's shirt tugged one side, smoothed a wrinkle on the other.

"I packed the lemon rice in the green tiffin. The one with the tighter lid. Aachi made it fresh, just for you. I also added an extra piece of coconut barfi. You'll eat it when you get nervous. I know you."

Vihaan tried to smile, but his throat was already beginning to ache with all the words he didn't know how to say. He reached for the plate in her hand, and she let go with hesitation as if passing it over meant admitting something.

Inside, Aachi sat on the floor by the window, her legs folded beneath her, a cloth spread across her lap. Her fingers, knotted with age but precise with purpose, were threading a garland of jasmine and orange kanakambaram. The flowers seemed to glow in the soft light warm embers of memory and scent. She didn't look up when Vihaan stepped in.

"You didn't wake the gods," she said.

Vihaan tilted his head, a smirk threatening to form. "I thought you already did."

A faint twitch of her lips betrayed her amusement. He sat beside her, cross-legged. The floor was cool and familiar, painted a deep red that had seen decades of feet and festivals.

"You know why we make garlands?" she asked, tying another knot. "No, Aachi." "One flower is beautiful," she said. "But short-lived. Together, they remember. Together, they mean something." He watched her hands, weathered and sure. The way she cradled each bloom, like it had a story to tell. She dipped her finger into the dabba of kumkum and pressed a dot to his forehead.

"Take all your pieces your silence, your stubbornness, your stories and string them tight. Don't lose any."

Vihaan didn't trust his voice, so he nodded.

Then, without ceremony, she slid a folded note into his palm and closed his fingers around it.

"Read this only after the train moves."

The Madgaon Railway Station was a slow explosion of noise and motion. Porters in red shirts weaved through crowds with luggage on their heads like balancing acts in a street circus. Chai vendors yelled over train horns, their voices curving through steam and smoke. Children clung to their mothers, their cries tangled with the shriek of brakes. Somewhere near Platform 3, someone's radio blared a devotional song, and from another corner, a hawker shouted about bhel puri with extra sev.

Vihaan stood in the middle of it all, holding his bag close to his chest, feeling like a punctuation mark out of place in a noisy sentence.

His father hadn't come to the station. That morning, just as Vihaan was slipping on his sandals, Appa had handed him a crisp 500-rupee note without looking up from the newspaper. He'd tucked it into Vihaan's palm like a secret.

"For something stupid," he'd mumbled. "Do something useless, at least once."

It was the closest his father had ever come to saying go enjoy your life.

His mother hadn't come either. She hated train stations; said they smelled like goodbyes that took too long. She'd stood in the doorway with her arms folded, eyes unreadable, as Vihaan stepped into the auto. But he knew she'd walk to the porch the moment he left, pick up his towel, and smell it like it was still him.

Only Aachi had insisted on coming. Of course she had.

Now she walked beside him, one hand holding up the edge of her saree, the other clutching a small cloth parcel a warm bundle that carried lemon rice, fried curry leaves, and the smell of home. She walked slowly, but every step was deliberate. She didn't speak much.

She didn't have to.

They reached Platform 4 just as the train began to hum in the distance a long, serpentine thing that approached with the weight of inevitability. Vihaan froze. His stomach tightened. His fingers went numb around the strap of his bag.

Aachi looked at him. Really looked.

"I don't know if I can do this," he whispered.

She didn't answer right away. She adjusted the pleats of her saree, shook the garland gently to remove any loose petals, and then stepped forward. Her hands, soft and steady, placed the garland over his neck, letting it settle like a blessing against his chest. Then she reached into his shirt pocket and pressed the folded letter deeper, as if it could reach his ribs.

"You've already done the hardest part," she said. "You stayed soft."

The train screeched to a full stop, metal and steam and motion. She stepped back without another word.

Vihaan climbed aboard.

And as the train pulled forward, he looked out the window saw her one last time. Not waving. Just standing there, hands folded, face calm. A thread of white hair loosened by the wind danced near her cheek. And then, like everything else, she disappeared into motion.

The train began with a tug not sharp, not sudden, but enough to tell the heart it had begun. Vihaan sank into his window seat, his bag tucked at his feet, the cloth parcel from Aachi resting carefully in his lap. The scent of curry leaves wafted from the knot, warm and familiar, like a hand on his shoulder.

Outside, the station peeled away like a slow illusion. The platform blurred. The people melted into each other. The red pillar near the tea stall disappeared. The sea, somewhere in the distance, sighed once more before vanishing completely.

Vihaan leaned his forehead against the glass.

The train compartment hummed with quiet life. A toddler in the opposite aisle sat cross-legged on her mother's lap, chewing on the corner of a biscuit like it held the secrets of the universe. A man with a thick mustache and thicker glasses snored softly into a book, his mouth slightly open as though dreaming of punctuation. Two college boys above Vihaan on the top berths were already arguing in Hindi about who had forgotten the charger. Their voices rose, fell, then broke into laughter.

Vihaan watched it all with the detachment of someone trying not to belong too quickly.

He stared at his own hands tanned, calloused from beach games and bicycle chains. They looked foreign now. He rubbed his thumb against a thin scar near his knuckle, a leftover from a fishhook incident he hadn't told anyone about.

A memory floated up: he and his cousin trying to catch crabs with a plastic bucket and a half-split coconut shell. They failed miserably, of course ended up chasing each other instead, covered in wet sand and mosquito bites. Aachi had scolded them both with a finger wag, then fed them extra appalam with dinner anyway.

Vihaan smiled faintly.

The train rumbled deeper into Karnataka now, past long stretches of green fields and sugarcane farms. A vendor passed through their compartment, chanting in a monotone rhythm: "Chai–chai–chai, kaapi, bonda–vadaa–chai."

Vihaan held up two fingers. "One tea, please." The man handed him a paper cup and a tiny plastic packet of sugar. The tea was watery, over-sweet, and possibly reheated twice. But it was hot. Vihaan cupped it like he used to cup sea foam, letting the warmth seep into his palms.

He didn't know anyone on this train.

And yet, somehow, he didn't feel completely alone.

He looked out the window again. Trees blurred. Hills passed like sleepy giants. Every few minutes, a child outside would wave at the train little brown hands flapping with abandon. Vihaan waved back once. Just once.

He thought about what Aachi had said: You stayed soft.

Maybe softness wasn't weakness.

Maybe it was the only thing that still made sense.

The train curved slowly around a bend, revealing a stretch of emerald hills layered with mist. The rhythmic clatter of the wheels had settled into something familiar like a lullaby whispered from below.

Vihaan reached into his shirt pocket.

The letter was still warm from his body heat, its corners slightly creased. He unfolded it carefully, as if opening something sacred. The paper smelled faintly of incense and sandalwood the scent of Aachi's room, of the puja corner with flickering lamps and yellow marigold garlands.

He read.

"Kanna, You're not just going somewhere. You're unfolding.

Like the tide that leaves only to return, you will carry our sand in your steps.

Do not fear the silence. It is only the sea, catching its breath.

You were born in a house that listens where the walls keep secrets, and the floor remembers your footsteps.

Take that quiet with you. Let it guide you when the world becomes too loud.

Bravery does not always shout. Sometimes, it hums. It waits. It chooses not to fight what it can understand.

Hold your kindness close. Let it walk ahead of you like a lantern.

You may forget the names of our lanes, the taste of ripe jackfruit, or the sound of the ceiling fan clicking in the night.

But never forget the warmth in your chest when someone truly sees you.

That is home.

You are not leaving us. You are widening us.

You are not alone. You carry a house in your chest, a porch in your breath, a prayer in your walk.

And when the city tries to make you forget, sit still.

The ocean inside you will always remember the way back.

With all the love this sea can hold,

Aachi"

Vihaan read it once.

Then again.

Each word settled into him like sand finding space between stones; soft, slow, inevitable. Her voice was in every syllable. Not as an echo, but a presence.

He remembered her stirring tea in the mornings, humming an old devotional song that didn't belong to any god in particular. He remembered her fixing the collar of his uniform, even when he told her it wasn't "cool." He remembered the way she once told him that the sea wasn't endless, just patient.

The letter folded back into his palm like a breath returning to the lungs.

He didn't cry. But something loosened in his chest like a knot gently untied.

The fields rolled by.

The wind curled around the edges of the window.

And in that moment, Vihaan didn't feel like he was leaving home.

He felt like he was carrying it.

The train had slipped into the leafy heart of Karnataka now, moving like an old poem through a forest of banyans and betel trees. The air outside was cooler, sweeter. Afternoon light draped over the fields like an old bedsheet soft, worn, and tinged with gold.

Vihaan's stomach growled.

He looked at the cloth bundle beside him green-checked, knotted tightly in a way only Aachi knew how. He untied it gently, like unfolding a memory. Inside was a round steel tiffin, still warm, holding lemon rice speckled with mustard seeds, fried curry leaves, and roasted peanuts. Alongside it, carefully wrapped in banana leaf, a wedge of coconut barfi that had already begun to sweat from the heat.

He paused.

He imagined Aachi's hands that morning patting the rice, tasting it with that old silver spoon, adding a final squeeze of lime like a secret ingredient. He could almost hear her muttering at the stove: "Too much salt and you'll dream of storms."

He smiled and took a bite.

The flavors exploded tangy, crunchy, soft. They didn't just feed his hunger. They filled something hollow inside.

Across the aisle, the toddler who had been munching on biscuits earlier was now wide-eyed and restless. Her mother struggled to keep her still, swaying and shushing gently.

Vihaan broke off a small piece of barfi and wrapped it in a tissue. He leaned across and offered it with a nod.

The mother looked unsure.

"It's homemade," Vihaan said softly. "By a grandmother who believes barfi solves everything."

She accepted it with a grateful smile.

The little girl took the piece carefully, then tucked her head into her mother's shoulder like a shy crab returning to its shell.

Vihaan returned to his food, still smiling. Not because of what he'd given but because it had reminded him that he still had something worth sharing.

He cleaned the steel tiffin with the edge of the banana leaf and placed everything back into the cloth bundle, knotting it neatly.

From the upper berth, one of the college boys dropped a headphone, and leaned down.

"Bhaiya, what did you eat? Smells like a five-star hotel inside a temple."

"Lemon rice," Vihaan replied.

"With what magic?" the boy asked, grinning.

Vihaan paused thoughtfully. "With a pinch of homesickness and a tablespoon of coconut bias."

They both laughed.

And in that brief exchange, Vihaan realized something: even here, among strangers and chai vendors and the smell of steel and sweat, he could still be himself. Quiet. Curious. Softly funny. Watching everything. Feeling more than he said.

By late afternoon, the light began to turn. Not fade, exactly but shift, like the slow pulling of a curtain made of gold. Outside the window, the fields transformed into shadowy pools, and the trees stood taller, their outlines deepening as if bracing for night.

Vihaan leaned into the windowpane, tracing his reflection in the glass. It stared back at him familiar and distant all at once. A boy on the edge of something. Not grief. Not joy. Just movement.

He looked down at his towel, now folded neatly in his lap. He hadn't used it since boarding. But its presence had become a kind of anchor soft, familiar, ridiculous in its own way. His roommate would probably laugh when he saw it. Call it a beach rag or a bedtime security blanket.

Let them.

Vihaan smiled to himself.

The train began to slow near a nameless village, halting for reasons no one explained. Outside, children ran barefoot beside the tracks, waving at the windows with the kind of unfiltered enthusiasm only childhood allowed. One boy held a kite made of old newspaper and string. It flapped and dove in the breeze, stubborn and wild.

Vihaan lifted his hand and waved back.

He didn't know why. It just felt right.

Behind him, a vendor entered with boiled corn in baskets and cucumber slices sprinkled with red chili salt. The train was a living, breathing organism people eating, stretching, snoring, whispering, offering opinions on cricket scores and marriage proposals.

And yet Vihaan remained wrapped in a kind of stillness. Not the heavy stillness of sorrow, but the gentle quiet that comes before rain. Before something begins.

He opened his sketchbook the one he carried since school and flipped to the last page. It was mostly blank, except for a rough pencil outline of his beach at home. Just a few lines and curves. Unfinished.

He pulled out his pen and beneath it, wrote:

"I don't know who I will become.

But today, I was brave enough to leave."

He paused.

Then underlined it.

Outside, the sky had turned a tender indigo, the first stars blooming like promises in the dark. The train began to move again, slowly at first, then with purpose a hum of steel against distance.

Vihaan closed his eyes and exhaled. He wasn't ready. But maybe that was never the point. Readiness wasn't a destination. It was a direction. A whisper in the chest that said: walk anyway. He curled into the window seat, towel beside him, sketchbook resting against his heart. And somewhere, softly, the sea he carried inside rolled forward.

CHAPTER TWO

BETWEEN THE STATIONS OF SILENCE

Morning on a train was different. Trains didn't carry just people. They carried pauses, unfinished thoughts, and goodbyes that hadn't found their words yet.

It didn't arrive in full color, or with a chorus of birds like at home. It crept in slow, diffused through cracked windows and dim bulbs. The compartment hummed with the breath of strangers passengers curled in awkward angles, mouths half-open, heads bobbing like tulsi leaves in temple water.

Vihaan stirred gently. He hadn't slept much, but he hadn't stayed awake either. The rhythm of the train had lulled him into a place between memory and dream. In that half-sleep, he thought he heard waves crashing against concrete. But there were no beaches here. Only track and steam. He remembered hearing his name maybe once, maybe twice but the voice wasn't anyone from the train. It had come from somewhere deeper. Maybe from the porch back home, maybe from a wave.

The sky outside was a dull silver now, and the fields had changed. No longer the lush, salt-laced greens of the coast these were drier, broader, coated with early fog. Crows flew low. Distant temples stood like forgotten songs, their domes catching the shy sun.

Vihaan shifted in his seat. The towel was still beside him, undisturbed. He rubbed his eyes and looked around.

The toddler across the aisle was now asleep, her small foot poking out from under a pink blanket. Her mother sipped chai in silence, eyes fixed out the window like she was searching for someone on the horizon. The college boys were still asleep above, one of them murmuring nonsense in his dreams.

The man with the newspaper now creased and drooled on had turned over completely, snoring into the armrest.

The quiet was strange. Not empty, but heavy. As if everyone was carrying thoughts too full to speak aloud.

Vihaan pulled out his sketchbook, flipping through pages filled with half-drawn boats, tiled rooftops, and the face of a girl he'd never shown anyone drawn from memory, stitched from glimpses.

He didn't draw now. Just held the book, as if its weight might balance the one in his chest.

Then, a sound: click, shfft. The train's sliding door opened at the far end of the coach. A man entered short, gray-haired, carrying a flute in his pocket like a pen. He passed through without a word, found a seat two rows ahead, and began humming.

Low. Melodic. Familiar.

It was a tune Vihaan hadn't heard in years one Aachi used to hum while sieving rice. Simple. Repeating. Comforting.

He sat up straighter. Something in his chest pulled tight, like a string being tuned.

Was it coincidence? Or memory playing tricks?

The man didn't look back. Just stared out the window and let the tune dissolve into the rattle of steel.

Vihaan closed his eyes again, not to sleep but to hold the sound a little longer. Outside, the train moved through silence.

And inside, a boy carried stories that had not yet been told.

The train clattered through a sleepy town that looked like it had forgotten to wake up. Rows of mud-colored homes blurred past, their verandas still empty, a few crows hopping around in search of leftovers. The platform that followed was deserted, save for a stray dog curled near a faded bench and a chai stall run by a man too sleepy to shout.

The train didn't stop. It just slowed like a yawn and then pushed forward again. Vihaan sat up straighter, the cold of the window lingering on his cheek. He rubbed his eyes and stretched gently, careful not to disturb the red towel folded beside him like a quiet companion. As he reached into his bag for a biscuit packet, his eyes met someone else's.

The girl across the aisle around his age, maybe a little older was sketching something on a page. Not a phone, not a book. A real page.

A real pencil.

She noticed his glance and gave a small nod the kind that wasn't an invitation, but also not a rejection.

Vihaan nodded back, a little too quickly.

He turned his eyes to the biscuit packet, suddenly more interested in it than he'd ever been. He fumbled with the wrapper for a moment longer than necessary, then broke off two pieces and placed one on the window ledge a habit from home. You always shared with the crows. Even if they weren't around.

"You think they'll find you here?" a voice asked.

He looked up. The sketching girl had spoken, eyes still on her drawing.

"Who?"

"The crows," she said, tilting her chin toward the biscuit. "Seems like an offering."

Vihaan chuckled, caught between embarrassment and amusement. "You never know. They're clever. Might've hitched a ride."

She smiled faintly. Then returned to her sketching.

Vihaan hesitated. He wanted to ask what she was drawing. He wanted to ask her name. But something held him back maybe it was the rhythm of the train, or maybe the kind of shyness that only surfaces in long-distance silence.

So instead, he turned to his sketchbook and opened a blank page.

And drew a crow on a train.

Wearing sunglasses.

He grinned at his own ridiculousness. Moments like these were gifts small, unspectacular, but full. A conversation that went nowhere. A glance that said, I see you. A biscuit left uneaten, just in case someone with feathers and memories decided to stop by.

He didn't need a full story. Not yet.

He hadn't expected a stranger to understand him through silence. But here she was sketching the same world he was trying to put into words. Sometimes, just the feeling that someone else saw the world like you did even for a second was enough.

The train rattled on.

And in his notebook, the crow gained a tiny backpack.

Sleep didn't come like a switch.

It arrived like sea mist soft, slow, wrapping around the edges of Vihaan's thoughts. The warmth of the train. The hum beneath him. The faint melody still lingering from the man's flute. Everything blurred.

His sketchbook slipped from his fingers onto his lap.

His breath deepened.

And suddenly, he was barefoot on the beach.

But it wasn't like home. The beach was too wide. The sky was violet.

The waves moved in reverse pulling inwards, not crashing out. He looked down, and his footprints trailed behind him. Hundreds. Maybe thousands. All his own.

The red towel was tied around his shoulders like a cape. It flapped gently in the wind. The sand under his feet wasn't warm. It pulsed. Like it remembered who he was.

Far in the distance, someone stood in the surf facing away. A woman in a pale blue saree, her hair braided with jasmine. She didn't move, but he knew exactly who she was.

"Aachi?" he called. No answer.

He ran. But the closer he got, the farther she seemed. The tide deepened, swallowing his steps. And still he ran, the towel trailing behind like a promise.

Then he heard it her voice, clear as temple bells.

"Swim. Fall. Float. Fight. But never, never stop."

The world blurred into gold. The sky cracked open like a coconut. And Vihaan fell forward into the water not cold, not heavy, just endless. He woke with a small gasp.

The train was still moving. A light drizzle had begun to trace fingers down the windows. The girl across the aisle was gone maybe in the washroom, maybe vanished like dreams do.

He sat up straighter, brushing his hair back, the dream still clinging to the inside of his ribs.

His sketchbook lay open. The crow drawing stared back at him, now smudged at the edges. He ran a thumb over it, not to fix it, but to feel something real.

Dreams weren't new to Vihaan.

But this one it didn't feel like fiction.

It felt like instruction.

He looked out at the rain, watching droplets race down the glass like they were trying to reach somewhere first. His reflection shimmered between them older, tired, but oddly lighter.

Somewhere behind him, someone sneezed. A phone rang. A baby cried.

But in his chest, there was only the sound of waves the kind that didn't crash, only called.

The rain had stopped, but it left the windows streaked and sleepylooking. The fields outside were bathed in post-shower quiet wet earth, washed leaves, buffaloes blinking with boredom.

Vihaan rubbed his eyes and sat up, adjusting his seat. His back ached from the strange angles he'd curled into while dozing. He reached for the bottle near his bag, took a sip of warm water, and looked around the compartment again.

That's when he noticed the old man across from him someone new.

He hadn't seen him board. Or perhaps he'd been there all along, like a tree you only notice once it rustles.

The man was thin, draped in an off-white veshti and a shawl that looked older than the train. His beard was more air than hair. And in his lap was an actual paper map creased, faded, patched with cellophane tape in corners.

Vihaan stared, quietly fascinated.

"Ever used one?" the man asked, without looking up.

Vihaan blinked. "A paper map? No. Only GPS."

"Hmm," the man hummed. "GPS tells you where you are. But a map tells you who you were planning to be."

Vihaan smiled, unsure if that was wisdom or mischief. That's the thing about wisdom. It never arrives loudly. It slips into your pocket and waits to be remembered.

"Where are you headed?" the old man asked.

"Mumbai," Vihaan said. "IIT. Civil Engineering."

The man nodded approvingly, as though that answered a different question altogether.

He folded the map slowly with the kind of care usually reserved for prayer flags and slipped it into a cloth satchel.

"You know what makes a good engineering?"

Vihaan hesitated. "Math?"

The man chuckled, eyes crinkling. "Math helps. But more than that... you must know how to listen to silence."

Vihaan tilted his head. "Silence?"

"Yes," the man said. "Buildings speak before people do. So do trains. And beaches. And houses where mothers stop calling your name but never stop setting your towel out."

Vihaan felt his throat tighten.

The man looked out the window and added gently, "Don't let the city make you forget the weight of small things."

They sat in quiet after that. Not awkward more like a pause between verses.

Then the man leaned back, pulled a woolen cap over his eyes, and said, "Wake me up if we pass a mistake."

Vihaan chuckled, quietly.

And somehow, in that strange, brief exchange, he felt lighter. Not braver, not smarter just more himself.

It reminded him of something Aachi once said while folding clothes:

"Some people enter your life like commas just long enough to make you breathe."

He looked at the man, now gently snoring, cap askew.

Vihaan exhaled, and the window fogged with the warmth of it.

The journey still had miles to go. But his heart felt less like it was leaving something behind and more like it was picking something up along the way.

It started with a single Parle-G biscuit.

One moment, the toddler from across the aisle was peacefully gnawing on it. The next, she dropped it face-down on the floor near Vihaan's feet. Her eyes widened in slow-motion horror.

Then came the gasp.

Not from her but from her older brother, seated beside her with a paper cone of murukku. He pointed at the biscuit like it was a crime scene.

"You dropped it! Now it's dead!"

"No it's not!" she screeched, diving for it.

The mother intervened, mildly flustered but practiced in this dance. "We don't eat things from the floor," she said with the weariness of someone who had said it every day for five years.

"But it was still smiling!" the toddler argued, waving the biscuit's half-crumbled face. "It wasn't ready!"

Across the row, a plump auntie in a bright green salwar kameez leaned in with gleeful commentary.

"Children today! We used to eat mud and still pass exams," she declared loudly, addressing no one and everyone. "This floor is cleaner than most kitchens!"

Someone snorted. Someone else applauded.

Vihaan, meanwhile, watched it all with silent amusement. The toddler, biscuit in hand, now leaned her head dramatically against her mother's arm and announced, "I miss my puppy."

"You don't have a puppy," her brother muttered.

The auntie gasped again. "No puppy? That's emotional neglect."

Laughter erupted.

The old man beside Vihaan stirred briefly beneath his cap, muttered, "Avoiding puppies is how we avoid heartbreak," and fell back asleep. Vihaan smiled wide, this time.

The compartment had transformed in minutes. From sleepy silence to a theater of chaos, emotion, and accidental comedy. No one had asked for it, but no one was complaining.

A college boy climbed down from the upper berth holding a packet of glucose biscuits. He bent, offered it to the toddler solemnly like a peace offering between kingdoms.

She considered it, sniffed once, then accepted without apology.

Balance restored.

Vihaan leaned back against the window, letting the laughter settle around him like warm cotton. He wasn't used to being in rooms or trains full of this kind of noise. But there was something comforting about it too.

This was life, raw and unscripted.

Spilled snacks. Loud aunties. Made-up puppies. And strangers becoming familiar in the space of a few shared moments.

Vihaan didn't say much.

But his eyes sparkled.

He reached for his sketchbook and made a quick doodle: a biscuit with wings, rising dramatically from the train floor like a fallen hero ascending into snack heaven.

He titled it: "The Martyrdom of Parle-G."

It wasn't the drawing that stayed with him. It was the laughter. Proof that even strangers could feel like a family when the world was ridiculous enough. The city ahead was still far. But moments like this absurd, small, human reminded him that no matter where you were, laughter found a way in.

Even on a floor that had probably seen things better left unsaid.

As the sun leaned westward, the train entered the outskirts of Mumbai a gradual unraveling of landscape and tempo.

Gone were the sugarcane fields and palm trees. In their place rose concrete pillars, rusted rooftops, tangled electric lines like veins stretched across the sky. The air changed too heavier with smog, denser with motion. Every minute, the train slowed slightly, groaned under its own weight, then moved again like a swimmer pushing through thick currents.

Around him, the compartment began to stir.

The college boys above repacked their bags with sleepy urgency, earbuds dangling like forgotten vines. The auntie adjusted her dupatta, reapplied lipstick in a compact mirror, and began giving unsolicited advice to no one in particular: "Mumbai is not for the slow. If you hesitate, someone will steal your turn. And your vada pav."

The toddler now wore sunglasses too large for her face and insisted she was a pilot.

Vihaan, meanwhile, sat still like the eye in a storm. His fingers rested on the towel folded neatly in his lap. He hadn't unfolded it once during the entire journey, but its fabric had become familiar under his fingertips like prayer beads for someone who didn't know the chants.

He looked out.

Skyscrapers began to peek through the haze. So did small tin homes, blue-tarp roofs, satellite dishes stacked like silver petals.

Mumbai didn't arrive all at once.

It emerged in layers color, steel, exhaustion, ambition.

It wasn't beautiful. But it pulsed with something alive.

Vihaan could feel it in his bones. A nervous drumbeat. A breath he'd held since boarding the train.

He imagined the station ahead: the platform packed, the signs large and foreign. A sea of bodies. The weight of newness.

But this time, he didn't feel like hiding.

He remembered Aachi's words: "You're not leaving home. You're widening it."

He reached into his sketchbook and scribbled a line:

"Some cities roar.

But I'll arrive like quiet rain."

He smiled at it. Not for what it meant but for what it felt like. He imagined her voice, not instructing, but watching. Like the sea always did. Always just close enough to catch him if he fell.

Behind him, the older man with the map stirred once more.

"We're close," he mumbled, rubbing his eyes.

Vihaan nodded.

The train gave a final groan, entering the shadow of the city's sprawl.

Mumbai waited.

And for the first time in hours, Vihaan sat upright, spine straight, eyes clear not because he was ready.

But because he wasn't afraid of not being.

Chhatrapati Shivaji Terminus rose into view like a fortress of time and noise.

The iron arches, stained glass, and gothic spires all stood noble and tired a cathedral built not for prayer, but for movement. As the train slid into the platform, its wheels screeched like a long-held breath finally released.

People surged.

Before the train even stopped fully, passengers scrambled for bags, shouted over each other, and bargained with porters in a cacophony that felt both rehearsed and uncontainable. The smell hit next a blend of petrol, sweat, frying batter, and something old, like rusted history baked under a hot sky.

Vihaan didn't rush.

He stood, slung his bag over his shoulder, and picked up the red towel like it was a sacred thread. He folded it carefully and tucked it between his sketchbook and his chest close enough to feel through his shirt.

The door opened with a hiss, and he stepped down.

Feet met stone.

And the city swallowed him.

No one looked at him. No one waited. He was just another face a boy with too-large eyes, holding too-small belongings in a station built for giants. A cart full of steel lunchboxes almost ran over his toes. A man yelled for a taxi. A woman in heels weaved through the crowd like she was late for something important and beautiful.

Vihaan paused.

Not because he was lost but because the world was suddenly too large for words.

Then, like the sea returning in whispers, he heard it.

Aachi's voice not outside, but within:

"The ocean only looks big because you haven't swum in it yet."

He breathed in.

Slowly.

And stepped forward.

He walked through the crowd, past newspaper boys, chipped tiles, peeling posters, and pigeons that didn't flinch. His fingers traced the strap of his bag like it was a rope tied to home.

When he reached the auto stand, the driver didn't even ask where. Just glanced at him and said, "IIT?"

Vihaan nodded.

"Powai?"

Another nod.

"Meter se jayenge," the driver said, already starting the engine.

As the auto weaved into traffic past honking taxis, men pushing carts of fruit, and walls covered in hand-painted movie ads Vihaan pressed his sketchbook to his lap and looked out.

The city didn't slow down for him.

But he didn't need it to.

He didn't arrive like a hero.

He arrived like rain quiet, persistent, and carrying the memory of where he came from.

Somewhere in his pocket, a pebble from his beach clicked gently with each turn.

And he smiled, not because he was ready. But because he knew He would begin, anyway.

CHAPTER THREE

THE ROOM WITH THE VIEW OF SOMEWHERE ELSE

The auto rickshaw sputtered to a halt in front of a long, faded building with half its nameboard covered by moss. A blueand-white sign above the arched entrance read:

"Hostel Block – 3, East Wing"

The "3" had been scratched so often it now resembled a 5 or a 2, depending on how you felt that day.

Vihaan stepped out slowly, like a guest at a stranger's wedding. He had imagined a hostel with history, maybe charm. But this one had stains that looked like they told stories, and none of them were romantic.

His legs were stiff. His shirt stuck to his back. The heat in Mumbai wasn't like home it didn't greet you. It leaned on you.

The rickshaw driver honked once, impatiently, and drove off before Vihaan could even say thank you. A pigeon flew down from the balcony and landed with the confidence of a tenant.

He looked up.

The building wasn't old in the romantic sense. It was old in the "we'll fix that after midterms" kind of way. Rusted grills. Water stains on corners. Wires spilling from walls like hair untied too fast.

Yet something about it didn't repel him. It had... presence.

He walked through the hallway, bag bouncing against his hip, red towel slung over his shoulder like a reluctant cape. Students passed him with practiced speed some carrying laptops, others holding chai cups like lifelines. No one stopped. No one stared.

He reached Room 17 on the first floor.

A small paper sign above the door read: "Welcome, Freshers (Don't die)."

He knocked. Silence.

He turned the knob and pushed the door open.

The room greeted him with the soft crunch of dust underfoot. It was... not large. Two narrow beds, one rusted ceiling fan that rotated with a squeaky revolution, a pair of wooden study desks one with initials carved deep into its edge: "YJ '18".

The window was open, but the curtain was caught on a nail and flapped uselessly like a flag with no country.

Vihaan dropped his bag and sat on the edge of the bed that faced the window. The mattress gave a tired sigh beneath him. It sank like it remembered every boy who had sat there and wondered if they belonged. Outside, he could see the edge of a cricket field, the back of another hostel block, and a lone dog scratching itself in philosophical circles.

It wasn't what he imagined.

But somehow, it was exactly what it needed to be.

He placed the towel on his pillow, then carefully took out his sketchbook and placed it on the table like a relic.

Then he sat still.

Letting the room breathe around him.

It didn't feel like home.

But it didn't ask him to pretend either.

And that, he thought, was a good beginning.

The door creaked open without a knock.

Vihaan looked up.

A tall boy with a half-buttoned shirt and headphones slung around his neck barged in, dragging a giant blue suitcase and a duffel bag that looked like it had lost a few wars.

"Yo! Room 17?" the boy asked.

Vihaan nodded. "Yeah."

"Nice," the boy said, dropping his bag with a thud loud enough to wake the dead or at least the ceiling fan, which responded with an annoyed squeak.

"I'm Nikhil," he said, holding out a hand as if they'd already agreed to be best friends. "Civil Engineering. From Nagpur. I snore like a foghorn and I have no shame."

Vihaan blinked. "Vihaan. Civil Engineering. From Goa."

Nikhil gave a mock salute. "Nice! Beaches, girls, seafood. Respect." Vihaan raised an eyebrow. "In that order?"

"Always," Nikhil grinned.

He moved like he was powered by caffeine and confidence, already unzipping his bag, tossing clothes onto the bed and pulling out a poster of Tony Stark that he began taping to the wall. The tape gave up halfway through and the poster drooped like it, too, wasn't ready for college.

As Nikhil organized his things with the chaos of someone rearranging a cyclone, the door creaked again this time slowly.

Another figure appeared.

This one was shorter, wore glasses slightly too big for his face, and carried a small backpack like it was made of glass.

He didn't speak.

He looked at Vihaan, nodded once, then at Nikhil, nodded again, and walked straight to the bed by the far wall.

Nikhil gestured. "That's Mukund. Don't take it personally I've known him since orientation. He speaks once a day. Usually to food."

Mukund was already unpacking methodical, precise. Toothbrush, pen stand, two neatly folded towels, one book: Linear Algebra and Its Applications. The most exciting thing in his bag was a spare battery pack. He unpacked like someone rehearsing for a life with no surprises.

Vihaan offered a polite smile.

Mukund nodded. It was probably his full vocabulary for the hour.

The room was now full not just of people, but sound and motion and newness. Vihaan could feel the air shift, as if the walls had expanded to make space for three different boys who didn't yet know how to coexist.

"Want chai?" Nikhil asked suddenly. "I heard the mess serves stuff that tastes like betrayal, but the corner shop has magic."

Vihaan hesitated.

Then nodded.

"Give me five," Nikhil said, already throwing on sandals and humming some old Bollywood song off-key.

As the door shut behind him, Mukund spoke soft, unexpected. "He's loud, but he won't let you feel alone."

Vihaan turned.

Mukund was already reading, his voice gone again.

But that single sentence lingered.

It was the kindest thing a stranger had said to him all day.

By late afternoon, the air had settled into a thick warmth that made the walls sweat and the ceiling fans spin like they were trying to stir soup. Vihaan needed to move. Not to go anywhere. Just to walk. To feel the weight of this place through the soles of his feet.

He stepped out of Room 17 with his towel slung around his neck a strange comfort blanket in the middle of concrete corridors.

The hostel courtyard was alive.

A group of boys played volleyball with more noise than skill, someone blasted Tamil kuthu songs from a third-floor window, and a guy wearing a Che Guevara tee sat under a tree, passionately arguing with no one about climate policy and hostel food.

Vihaan watched it all like a visitor at an exhibit titled: "How to Live Loudly."

As he turned the corner near the mess hall, he nearly collided with a student covered in paint blue splotches on his arms, glitter in his hair, and one sock missing entirely.

"Sorry!" the guy yelled, not at Vihaan, but to the universe in general, before jogging off with a bucket in one hand and a poster that read "FRESHERs NIGHT IS NOT A THREAT."

A nearby bench hosted two seniors mid-interrogation of a first-year boy who looked like he might dissolve if asked another question about his favorite author.

Vihaan didn't stop walking.

He passed notice boards cluttered with flyers: debate club auditions, dance team tryouts, a poetry group called Metaphorically Yours, and an ad for a civil engineering workshop titled "Beams and Dreams."

He paused at that one. The title made him smile. It was exactly the kind of thing Aachi would've loved something practical dressed in poetry.

He kept walking, past the main quadrangle, where a group of girls sat in a circle, sketchbooks open, pencils darting like dragonflies. The campus was a mosaic fragments of ambition, stress, laughter, sweat, and curiosity laid over each other with no glue. Just gravity. Vihaan didn't feel like a piece of the mosaic yet. More like a tile waiting to find where it fit.

Eventually, Vihaan found himself by the edge of the lake inside campus Powai Lake, they called it. It wasn't exactly the sea. But it had water, birds, ripples, and silence. That was enough for now. He imagined what Aachi might say. Probably that water is water, as long as it reflects the sky.

He sat down under a peepal tree.

From here, he couldn't see the hostels or the people. Just water.

He closed his eyes and listened.

The chirping of crickets. The occasional honk from a distant road. A crow cawed like it was late to something.

He imagined for a moment that the waves would speak back, like at home. But this lake didn't know his name yet.

Still, it didn't feel hostile.

Just... waiting. Like a blank page.

Vihaan smiled, faint and full.

He didn't need answers yet.

He just needed space to breathe.

The mess hall was not built for grace.

Its ceiling was high, its lights too white, and its fans spun in odd rhythms one faster, one slower, one that creaked like it had opinions about everyone's food choices. Long metal tables stretched in neat rows, each surrounded by red plastic chairs that looked like they came from a wedding and stayed forever.

Vihaan stood near the entrance, tray in hand, absorbing the chaos.

There were at least four serving counters. Each with their own line. Each with signage that made things more confusing: "VEG 1," "VEG 2," "SPL VEG," and a mysterious "DIET."

He joined a line arbitrarily.

In front of him, a boy complained that the rasam tasted like regret. The server replied, deadpan, "That's because it was boiled with broken dreams."

Vihaan tried not to laugh. He wasn't sure if it was a joke or a warning.

He finally reached the counter and was handed a plate with rice that clumped like it missed home, a curry of indeterminate color, and a scoop of what might have been curd or ambition, depending on the angle.

He took a seat at the corner of a long table.

Nikhil plopped down beside him seconds later, his tray piled with three rotis, two samosas, and a dangerously red chutney.

"Welcome to the battlefield," Nikhil grinned. "Eat fast, or the spoons run out."

Mukund followed, expression unchanged, carrying a tray that looked like it had been portioned with surgical precision.

"Tip," Nikhil added. "Avoid the purple pickle. It's fermented chaos."

Vihaan poked at his curry with the back of his spoon. It jiggled in defiance.

"I think mine just blinked," he said.

Nikhil snorted. "Then it's fresher than usual."

Despite the strangeness, Vihaan took a bite. It was... edible. Spicy in a way that sneaked up on you. His throat warmed, his eyes watered slightly.

Across the table, a boy tried to balance his tumbler on his forehead. Another was passionately explaining his startup idea that involved drone-delivered biryani. Someone else had drawn a caricature of a professor using ketchup on the table.

Vihaan quietly soaked it all in.

It wasn't elegant.

It wasn't familiar.

But it was alive.

And something about that felt oddly comforting.

He finished half his plate, sipped water from a steel tumbler that tasted vaguely of soap, and leaned back.

Nikhil was telling a story now something about a dog chase, a broken flip-flop, and an overripe mango that became a projectile.

Even Mukund chuckled.

Vihaan smiled. He didn't understand everything. But he liked that he didn't need to.

No one asked about Goa. No one asked if he missed home. But for a few minutes, the table buzzed with warmth.

He didn't love the food.

But he liked the feeling.

And that, he figured, was a start.

The hostel at night didn't sleep.

It buzzed not with noise, but with presence. The kind that lives in whispers behind closed doors, in muffled laughter under bedsheets, in ceiling fans that click like they're counting secrets.

Room 17 was quiet, but not still.

Nikhil had fallen asleep instantly, one arm over his face, headphones still loosely wrapped around his neck, snoring like a man auditioning for thunder.

Mukund read under a tiny clip-on lamp, eyes darting silently across the page. At exactly 10:59 p.m., he shut the book, folded his glasses, and climbed into bed without a sound a ritual rehearsed to the second.

Vihaan sat by the window, legs folded, notebook open on his lap.

The breeze that entered wasn't sea wind. It smelled of dust, rainsoaked stone, and distant kitchens preparing morning batter. But it moved gently, and that was enough.

He looked out.

Beyond the dim yellow glow of the hostel lights, the lake shimmered like a memory trying to stay awake. The silhouettes of trees swayed lazily, and somewhere far off, a fox cried a strange, melodic sound that made the night feel like it was listening.

Vihaan picked up his pen and wrote.

"It's not home.

But there's a towel by my pillow.

A sketchbook by my hand.

And a voice that tells me I am still me."

He paused.

Then, on a fresh line:

"Homesickness isn't loud.

It hums.

Like old lullabies in strange languages."

He closed the notebook gently, like putting a child to sleep.

Beside his bed, he unfolded the towel carefully smoothing out the edges and laid it over the pillow. It still held the faintest trace of salt.

Not sea salt. But memory.

He lay down.

Outside, someone dropped a bucket in the hallway. A group of boys burst into sudden laughter near the staircase, then dissolved into hushes. Water dripped from a leaking tap like the world ticking slowly forward.

Vihaan stared at the ceiling.

Not scared.

Not sad.

Just aware of how far he'd come, and how quietly the change was happening.

He turned to his side, pulling the edge of the towel close to his chin. The ceiling fan groaned again, reluctantly.

And somewhere, in that narrow space between ache and acceptance, he smiled.

Because this, he thought this strange, broken, buzzing place

Would soon begin to remember his name.

The next evening, just after dinner, Vihaan stepped out of the hostel with his phone clutched tight in his hand.

He didn't head to the courtyard or the lake. He found a quiet spot near the east wall of the hostel a place with patchy reception but fewer people, fewer eyes. The brick wall behind him still held the heat of the day. The air smelled of dry leaves and the tail-end of someone's incense stick nearby.

He dialed the number he'd memorized before he could write his own name.

It rang once.

Then twice.

And then

"Allo, kanna?"

Aachi's voice filled his ears like warm steam from a freshly opened tiffin. Cracked at the edges, sweet in the middle.

He couldn't speak at first.

So she did.

"You've reached safely? Room okay? Food edible?"

Vihaan nodded instinctively, then realized the futility. "Yes, Aachi. Room's fine. Food... happens."

She chuckled. "Don't let your bones dry out. Drink hot water. Carry eucalyptus. Mumbai's weather is a shapeshifter."

He closed his eyes.

It was incredible how she made advice feel like lullabies.

He imagined her sitting cross-legged on the porch, hair braided, an old mug of coffee beside her, the sea humming its own reply just behind.

"Your mother wants to speak," she said suddenly. "But first—one thing."

He waited.

"Have you cried yet?"

Vihaan froze.

There was no judgment in her voice. No teasing. Just a knowing softness like she had sent the question through layers of silence to land gently on his chest.

"No," he said, though he wasn't sure it was entirely true.

"Hmm," she said. "Then keep a towel near. Salt comes suddenly. Like the sea pulling tide when no one is watching."

Before he could answer, the phone rustled, and his mother's voice took over.

"Vihaan? Are you eating properly? Are you safe? Did your train have clean blankets?

Are your roommates... decent?" "All of the above, Amma," he smiled.

There was a pause.

Then, her voice smaller: "I put your towel in your bag. The one you used after playing football in the rain. I didn't want to say... I didn't want you to think we were making this too hard."

He leaned against the wall, eyes closed.

"I knew," he whispered.

Another pause.

Then she said, "Aachi talks to your towel every morning. Just so you know."

He laughed, a soft, warm sound that bounced against the bricks behind him.

They didn't say I miss you. That was not their language.

But when Aachi came back on and said, "Tell your building not to let you disappear. Or I'll come climb it myself,"

—he felt loved.

He hung up a few minutes later, heart heavier but steadier.

And as he walked back to Room 17, a breeze rustled through the trees not coastal, not salty.

But still... familiar.

The sky above IIT Bombay darkened slowly, not with drama, but with a soft dimming like someone was turning down the volume on the day.

Vihaan returned to Room 17 to find it bathed in the dull glow of the desk lamp. Nikhil was snoring again, sprawled like he'd fallen from the sky and made peace with it. Mukund sat cross-legged on his bed, headphones in, blinking slowly like a monk in sleep mode.

Vihaan entered quietly, kicked off his sandals, and sat on his bed. The towel, now folded neatly at the head, felt like an old friend watching over him. He picked it up, pressed it lightly to his face the faintest scent of the sea still clung to its fibers, like memory refused to wash off.

He opened his sketchbook.

The pages had begun to fill without him noticing the crow in sunglasses from the train, the outline of Room 17, a half-drawn bench by the lake. His lines weren't perfect, but they were his.

He flipped to a fresh page and began to draw the hostel building. Not as it was, but as it felt. Slightly hunched. Slightly wise. A bit too tall for its age. A structure that held secrets and late-night noodles and unshed tears in pillowcases.

He added a single window with a boy staring out: not sad, not excited. Just... aware. Drawing was the only way he knew how to explain what his heart noticed before his head did.

Then he scribbled beneath it:

"Some rooms are not built with walls.

They are stitched slowly with silence and toothbrushes and towels that remember."

He closed the book.

And started rearranging his desk.

Not in a rush. Just little things: placing his sketchbook at the center, tucking Aachi's letter into the side pocket of his bag. He placed a pebble the one from the beach at the edge of the windowsill. It didn't catch light. But it caught something else.

A feeling.

By the time he slipped under his sheet, the room had shifted.

Not in appearance.

But in presence.

It had begun to carry his shape.

The fan spun above with its usual tired rhythm. Nikhil snorted in his sleep. Mukund clicked off his playlist. The building groaned once as if settling its joints for the night.

Vihaan closed his eyes, towel tucked beneath his head, a small smile forming without permission.

He was still homesick.

But tonight, the ache felt like a candle warm, quiet, full of memory. And as he drifted into sleep, the room did not feel unfamiliar anymore.

It felt like it had started listening.

CHAPTER FOUR

THE PLACES WE PRETEND TO BELONG

The lecture hall looked more like a small stadium. Tiered rows, whiteboards taller than windows, and a projector that dangled from the ceiling like it wasn't quite sure it wanted to stay. Fans churned lazily above, circulating air thick with expectation and freshly ironed shirts.

Vihaan walked in clutching a new notebook pages too crisp, cover too bright. He chose a seat somewhere in the middle. Not too front to be seen. Not too back to be forgotten. He wasn't centre stage. But he wasn't in the wings either.

The hall filled quickly.

Some students sat in groups, voices loud and familiar. Others like him solo, scanning the room as if trying to find an exit even before the class began.

"Civil Engineering 101," said a voice that cracked through the static of the microphone like dry thunder.

A professor in a cream shirt and suspenders stepped to the podium with a kind of practiced exhaustion. His name was scrawled on the board in thick strokes: Dr. P. G. Menon.

"The basics," he said, tapping the chalk like a metronome. "Structures. Strength of materials. Fluid mechanics. Bridges. Buildings. Dreams built from dust."

That last line made Vihaan pause.

He wasn't sure if it was metaphor or muscle memory.

Around him, pens scratched. Pages turned. Someone beside him whispered, "Bro, what even is a modulus of elasticity?" and someone behind replied, "Whatever it is, mine's broken already."

Vihaan smiled, half by accident.

He opened his notebook but didn't write. Not yet.

He watched.

The professor scribbled a formula on the board — dense, elegant, confusing. Chalk dust floated in the sunlight like powdered thought.

Vihaan didn't know what the symbols meant. But he was drawn to the way they stood on the board. How they dared to claim space. Curved, stern, unapologetic. They were like footprints in a land he didn't know yet.

He let his eyes wander. He didn't want to memorise them yet. He wanted to understand how they felt in the bones of a building.

One student had color-coded their notes in four shades of neon. Another was asleep with their eyes open a skill, really. A boy in the front row wore formal shoes and sat ramrod straight like he was applying for the position of gravity.

Vihaan felt completely unqualified to be here.

But also strangely okay with it.

He didn't understand most of what was said.

But he understood what it felt like to want to.

And that, for now, was enough.

When the bell rang, it wasn't a sound it was a release. Dozens of bodies stood up like flowers unfolding too quickly. The rustle of bags, the clatter of bottles, the buzz of relief.

Vihaan stood too, notebook still empty, thoughts not.

He didn't rush out.

He stayed for a few seconds, watching the chalk marks blur as someone wiped the board clean.

It didn't erase what had been taught.

It just made space for what came next.

The café on campus wasn't much of a café.

It was a half-covered open-air canteen with steel tables, chipped benches, and a menu board held together by more tape than trust. A fan swung overhead with no intention of offering breeze to anyone. But it served hot samosas, questionable noodles, and tea that made you forget who you were for a few seconds.

Nikhil waved him over. "Come on, meet the circus."

Vihaan approached cautiously.

Around the table sat five other students; two girls, three boys each louder than the next. One wore sunglasses despite it being past 5 p.m. Another was in a kurta that looked stolen from an art festival. The third was dramatically re-enacting a scene from a Shah Rukh Khan movie using a samosa as a phone.

"This is Vihaan," Nikhil announced with flair. "My roommate. From Goa. Civil. Silent but spicy."

One of the girls curly-haired, nose ring, eyes like they'd seen five lives already grinned. "You draw, right? I saw you sketching during orientation."

Vihaan blinked. "Maybe."

"Definitely," she smirked. "You made that crow in sunglasses. Iconic."

Vihaan felt his ears warm.

The others laughed. Not unkindly just in that way where the world didn't pause for shyness.

The conversation swirled around him memes he hadn't seen, shows he hadn't watched, politics he hadn't followed, and crushes he hadn't even noticed. Someone mentioned a professor who wore two different shoes to class. Another claimed to have ghosted three people before lunch.

Vihaan nodded occasionally. Smiled politely. Bit into his samosa and let the chilli hit him like surprise truth.

Every now and then, someone would loop him in.

"What's Goa like?"

"Do you surf?"

"Are you one of those quiet boys who secretly writes poetry?"

"Do you believe in horoscopes?"

"What's your biggest architectural inspiration?"

He corrected them gently. "Civil, not architecture."

"Ah," one replied. "So you'll build bridges, not cathedrals."

Vihaan smiled. "Bridges are more useful."

They laughed again not at him, but around him. And somehow, that was easier to handle.

He didn't speak much. But he listened like a second language.

Every gesture, every pause, every accidental glance he noticed it all. The way the curly-haired girl kept adjusting her sleeves when nervous. The boy with the art-kurta only laughed when someone else did first. Even Nikhil, for all his volume, kept glancing at his phone too often, like waiting for something that wouldn't come.

Vihaan didn't belong.

Not yet.

But something in his chest some small, soft corner whispered: You will.

It happened between two moments the kind you almost miss because the world doesn't slow down for small magic.

Vihaan was walking back from the library, a thin volume of Structural Concepts for First Years tucked under his arm, when he saw her.

The girl from the train.

She was sitting alone on a cement bench under a neem tree near the Civil Department building legs folded, a sketchbook balanced on one knee, pencil dancing.

The same loose braid. The same blue-ink smudge near her wrist. A presence that didn't shout to be seen but somehow commanded it anyway.

She didn't notice him at first.

Vihaan froze mid-step, one foot still in the air like a paused scene.

And then

She looked up.

Their eyes met.

Not like strangers passing each other in hallways. Not like classmates seated three rows apart. But like two versions of the same quiet had collided again unsure whether to greet each other or let silence do the talking.

She tilted her head slightly.

Vihaan raised his eyebrows a shy half-smile tucked into the gesture.

Her lips twitched. Not a full smile. But something between I remember you and don't ruin this by speaking too soon.

Vihaan took a few steps forward, unsure whether he would stop or walk past.

He stopped.

Close enough to hear the scratch of her pencil on the page.

She didn't cover her sketch. She didn't look away either.

"I was starting to think you were a dream," Vihaan said, voice softer than the breeze.

"I thought you were mute," she replied, deadpan.

He laughed quick, breathy, real.

She glanced back at her page. "You always watch the world like you're sketching it with your eyes."

"That's because I usually am," he said.

A pause.

A crow landed near them, hopping with comical dignity, eyeing the pencil like it was a threat.

"Vihaan," he said finally, offering a name like a secret.

She didn't offer hers in return.

Instead, she said, "I liked your crow. The one with the sunglasses." Vihaan blinked. "I didn't think anyone noticed."

"I did," she said, standing now, sketchbook under one arm. "I notice things."

And with that, she walked away.

No introduction. No ending.

Just a trail of curiosity and sandalwood scent.

Vihaan stood still for a moment longer, his pulse strangely present in his fingertips.

He didn't chase the moment.

He let it settle inside him like light through dust slow, golden, and quietly transforming everything it touched.

The classroom buzzed with the pre-lecture ritual bags thudding against desks, bored yawns, whispered gossip. A boy two rows behind Vihaan whispered about bunking and heading to Marine Drive. Another cursed his alarm clock for not going off though, judging by his bed-head, it never stood a chance.

Vihaan sat at his usual seat, middle-left row, third from the window.

Not hidden. Not seen.

He opened his notebook just as Dr. Menon walked in, carrying a sheaf of stapled papers like they were a stack of judgment.

"No lectures today," he announced. "We're doing a surprise quiz."

The room groaned in unison like a temple full of hearts breaking gently.

"Relax," Dr. Menon said dryly. "It's five questions. I'm not testing what you know. I'm testing what you noticed."

That caught Vihaan's attention.

He took the sheet when it reached him, stared at the printed pencil questions. At first glance, they looked like a foreign language.

Define dead load and live load.

Explain the significance of Young's Modulus.

Draw the free-body diagram for a cantilever beam with uniform loading.

Identify the material best suited for foundation design in coastal areas.

Why do we test materials beyond their elastic limits?

Panic rippled quietly through the room.

Vihaan took a deep breath.

And thought about the lecture not the notes, but the rhythm of it.

How Dr. Menon had drawn the cantilever with a single sweep. How he'd used a brick as a metaphor. How he'd said:

"Civil engineers don't build. They understand where a structure wants to stand."

Vihaan wrote slowly.

Not perfectly.

But with attention.

He drew carefully, annotated in the margins. When he reached the coastal foundation question, he remembered Aachi telling him once, "You don't build coconut trees in marshland. Their roots know where they can't belong."

He smiled.

Clay-rich soils. Deep-piled foundations. Anchored footing. It made sense.

He finished just as the timer ran out. Nikhil beside him looked like he'd aged three years.

"What was that," Nikhil muttered, "an ambush from hell?"

Vihaan shrugged. "It wasn't too bad."

Dr. Menon walked past, collecting sheets. His eyes paused on Vihaan's just a second longer than necessary.

He didn't say anything.

But he didn't have to.

That look brief, unreadable, quietly approving was enough to light something small inside Vihaan's chest.

He stepped out into the hallway, sun sharp on his face, breeze hot and fast.

He hadn't topped the class. He hadn't outshone anyone.

But he had survived something unplanned.

And done it with care.

In a world that rushed past every feeling, that was its own kind of success.

Two days before the festival, the hostel transformed into a canvas of color and chaos.

Fairy lights twisted around stair railings like shy serpents. Paper lanterns swayed from balconies. Voices echoed down hallways —

laughter layered over shouting, bursts of music spilling out of rooms as students tested speakers and rehearsed dances.

Someone on the third floor had already lit sparklers indoors, setting off a minor fire alarm and major applause.

Nikhil was in full swing.

He'd somehow appointed himself the unofficial Decoration Commander of Hostel Block 3, barking instructions with a ruler in hand and glitter on his cheeks.

"Where's the tape? I need at least three more diyas per window!"

Mukund, surprisingly, was cutting rangoli stencils with surgical precision, his expression as intense as if solving a structural equation.

Vihaan stood near the door, watching the flurry, his hands deep in his pockets.

It wasn't that he disliked festivals.

Back home, he'd help string mango leaves across their porch while Aachi stirred payasam in the kitchen, the scent of cardamom thick in the air. His mother would hum old Tamil film songs and his father would wear his only white veshti with a safety pin that always came undone.

Here... there were lights, yes.

But none of them knew his name.

Nikhil tossed him a pack of string lights. "Here wrap these around the window grill."

Vihaan nodded, took them, but didn't move.

His chest felt too tight. His throat too full.

He slipped out without a word.

Outside, the campus had quiet corners if you knew where to look.

He walked aimlessly past the admin block, past the food court now half-lit like a memory mid-fade, until he reached the far side of the lake. A small concrete bench sat under an overgrown gulmohar tree, glowing orange with flowers.

He sat.

Didn't check his phone.

Didn't sketch.

Just... sat.

The water in the lake was still, dark, save for the moon caught in its reflection — blurred, unbothered.

Somewhere far, a flute played. Soft. Wandering.

And Vihaan let the ache expand.

Not the kind that brings tears.

The kind that hollows the chest with a gentleness you can't explain. He missed Aachi's voice calling his name while burning camphor.

Missed the way his mother overfed guests and his father nodded through every ritual like he understood Sanskrit better than the priest.

He didn't want to be dramatic.

He just wanted... proximity.

To the people who made silence feel sacred.

He leaned back, eyes tracing the curve of a star overhead.

A breeze passed.

Not the sea breeze of home. But kinder than usual.

And for the first time since arriving, Vihaan whispered a prayer.

Not to a god.

But to his own heart.

"Please hold me through this. Quietly."

It was nearly midnight when Vihaan returned to the room.

The festivities had faded into a softer hum distant music, muffled bursts of laughter, and the occasional whoop from a firecracker gone rogue. Room 17 was dim. Mukund was already asleep, earplugs in, blanket folded so perfectly it could've been a tutorial.

Nikhil was lying on his back, headphones resting on his chest, eyes open, staring at the ceiling like it was telling him secrets.

Vihaan moved quietly, but Nikhil spoke before he could even set his bag down.

"You ever feel like... you're the only one who's not sure they belong here?"

Vihaan froze.

He hadn't expected it not in Nikhil's voice, not in that hour, not from someone who spent his days shouting about samosas and playing air guitar with a broomstick.

But he answered honestly.

"Yeah," Vihaan said. "All the time."

Silence stretched between them.

Then Nikhil sat up, cross-legged on his bed, rubbing his neck like the truth had been weighing on it all evening.

"I was the first in my family to even finish 12th properly," he said. "My dad runs a hardware shop. We sell bricks. Actual bricks."

Vihaan leaned against his bedframe, towel across his lap like a soft habit.

Nikhil continued. "When I got into IIT, my chacha said, 'Don't forget where you come from.' But the truth is... I don't think I fit here. I can't speak English like some of the others. I've never watched half the shows they talk about. And group projects? I pretend to know what I'm doing. But inside " He stopped, laughed quietly, "I feel like a fly that crashed the party."

Vihaan didn't say anything immediately.

He just listened.

And that, Nikhil must've realized, was enough.

"I cover it up," he added. "Jokes. Loud music. I make people laugh before they notice I don't understand what they're laughing at."

There it was.

Truth — raw, cracked, unfiltered.

Not dramatic.

Just real.

Vihaan finally spoke. "You're not the only one."

Nikhil looked over.

Vihaan added, "I walk into rooms and scan for exits before I find the board. I double-check every word before I say it. And most days, I feel like I'm playing a character hoping no one calls me out."

Nikhil exhaled. "So we're both faking it?"

"Maybe," Vihaan said. "But maybe we're also... building something. Quietly."

A pause.

Then Nikhil nodded, slowly. "That's the most civil-engineering answer I've ever heard."

They both laughed.

It wasn't loud.

It wasn't forced.

It was shared.

And when the room fell quiet again, it wasn't empty.

It was earned.

A new silence. A friendly one.

Like bricks slowly understanding how to become a wall.

The lights were strung like stars who'd decided to stay low for the evening.

They crisscrossed the common room ceiling flickering in mismatched colors, swaying with every shift in wind and beat. A Bluetooth speaker crackled to life with old Bollywood remixes and one heartbreak anthem no one admitted they knew the lyrics to.

It was fresher's night but without a script.

Someone had hung a banner made of chart paper that read: "WELCOME TO HELL, BUT FUN."

Mukund corrected the spelling with a marker. Nikhil called it "modern sarcasm."

The room was crowded, warm, full of badly timed claps and overconfident voices. Vihaan stood near the edge of the chaos, sipping orange Rasna from a cracked steel tumbler. He hadn't planned to stay long.

But then the dancing began.

Not the kind you post on Instagram. The kind that defies rhythm and embraces the ridiculous. Boys stomping in slippers, trying to match steps. Someone did the hook step from "Lungi Dance" with the seriousness of a cultural performance. Another attempted breakdancing and pulled a muscle.

Vihaan found himself laughing.

Not the polite kind.

The real kind where your stomach tightens and your eyes crinkle and for a few seconds you forget why you were ever afraid to be seen.

"Come on!" Nikhil shouted, grabbing his wrist.

Vihaan shook his head.

"Don't be Goa-cool. One dance. Just flail. No one's judging Mukund's already doing kathak."

Sure enough, Mukund was twirling dramatically with a dupatta someone had tossed at him, wearing an expression that said, "I regret everything, but also nothing."

Vihaan stepped forward.

He didn't flail.

He flowed. Awkwardly. But sincerely.

He moved like someone remembering what joy felt like in their limbs.

And somewhere between the shoulder shimmy and the imaginary dhol beat, something shifted.

Not in the room. In him.

A crack in the weight he carried. A space for laughter to live. For the first time since he left home, he didn't feel like he was borrowing the moment.

He felt inside it.

Whole.

Someone tapped a spoon against a steel plate. "Speech from the freshers!" they yelled.

Groans. Whistles. Laughter.

Vihaan stepped back toward the wall, heart racing, hoping no one pointed to him.

Nikhil stepped forward instead, raised his glass of Rasna, and shouted, "To bridges!"

A few claps.

"To failing quizzes!"

More cheers.

"To surviving Hostel 3!"

Roar.

Then he turned, looked right at Vihaan, and added: "And to boys who carry oceans inside them quietly."

Silence.

Then: thunderous applause.

Vihaan didn't know whether to laugh or disappear.

He chose to smile fully.

Because maybe, for the first time...

He wasn't pretending to be here. He was.

CHAPTER FIVE

BLUEPRINTS OF BECOMING

The classroom smelled of chalk dust and ambition. He'd come to learn formulas, not feel the floor shake with memory. Not the loud, eager kind but the quiet kind, like books that had been read too many times and desks that remembered the elbows that leaned on them.

Vihaan walked in five minutes early. Not by habit by instinct. Something about this particular class made his chest feel tight and his hands oddly cold.

Introduction to Structural Design: Residential Spaces.

Dr. Rao stood at the front glasses hanging from a string, hair tied in a bun that looked like it had survived a wind tunnel. She was the kind of professor who didn't need to raise her voice to command attention. Her presence did the talking.

She placed a roll of blueprints on the desk and unrolled them like a secret being revealed.

"Your first assignment," she said, tapping the plan with her index finger, "is to design a basic residential layout."

Some students exhaled with visible relief. A few grinned. A couple high-fived like they'd been handed extra vacation days.

Vihaan just sat still.

"A house," she continued, "with two bedrooms, one common living area, a small kitchen, and the kind of bathroom that doesn't require divine intervention to fit into."

Laughter.

But her next words silenced it.

"Don't think this is easy. Designing a structure isn't about lines. It's about life. Walls hold space. But they also hold story. Every window you draw is a decision. Every angle, a question."

Vihaan's pen twitched in his hand.

She looked up, eyes scanning the room.

"I don't want symmetry. I want sincerity. Give me something that breathes."

Something in Vihaan's chest pulled taut like a curtain drawn too fast.

She handed out the brief: layout dimensions, functional criteria, submission deadline. Two weeks. Enough time to overthink everything. As the paper reached his desk, Vihaan stared at it.

Two bedrooms. Living area. Kitchen. Bathroom.

But all he could think of was the salt stains on the wall of Aachi's kitchen. The way the porch light flickered like it couldn't make up its mind. The single nail by the entrance where his father hung his key ring always clinking like it was glad to be home.

A house wasn't walls.

It was presence.

He looked around. Students were already talking in excited clusters comparing drafts in their heads, discussing optimal layouts, arguing about cross-ventilation.

Vihaan didn't join them.

He packed the brief into his folder, slung his bag over one shoulder, and stepped out into the sunlight blinking like someone who'd seen something they weren't sure they understood yet.

It wasn't the project that unnerved him. It was what the project might uncover.

He had come here to build.

But he hadn't realized he'd be building from within.

Vihaan spread his tools on the desk in Room 17 with ritualistic care — pencil, scale, T-square, eraser, the blank white sheet that dared him to begin.

He stared at it for ten minutes.

Then fifteen.

The page remained empty.

Not because he didn't know what to draw but because he knew exactly what he wanted to, and wasn't sure he should.

He leaned back, let the edge of the chair creak under him, and closed his eyes.

And just like that, he was back there.

Not in IIT.

But on that worn red-oxide floor where the breeze always smelt of turmeric and tide.

Their home hadn't been symmetrical.

It bent in odd places. The living room opened straight into the kitchen, separated only by a faded curtain with dancing elephants stitched into the hem. The bathroom door squeaked like an old gate. Aachi's bedroom had a sloped ceiling, low enough that she often joked, "Even thoughts have to bend in here."

But it worked not in the way rules said it should, but in the way comfort demands.

Each room knew its purpose. That house didn't need design. It knew what to hold and what to let go.

The porch, for example, wasn't just for shoes and rain-soaked umbrellas it was where his father read the paper with one leg up. It was where Vihaan had sat cross-legged, eating mangoes with both hands and no shame.

And the window beside the dining table the small one with the uneven grill was where Aachi whispered to the sea.

At night, the house breathed.

You could hear it in the ceiling's soft sighs, in the way water dripped rhythmically into the kitchen bucket, in the slow turning of the fan that tried its best despite age.

Every crack was familiar. Every shadow had its season.

He remembered how he used to sketch the floor plan as a child not to scale, but to story. He'd add arrows: "Here is where Aachi dropped her jasmine." "Here is where Amma makes noise but says she didn't." "Here is the cool tile where I slept when it was too hot to dream."

It wasn't architecture.

It was ancestry.

Back in the present, Vihaan opened his eyes.

The page still waited.

This time, his pencil moved not with confidence, but with memory. A rectangle first. Then a smaller one tucked beside it.

He didn't draw it exactly like his old house.

But he let it echo through the layout the open curve of the main hall, the kitchen angled just so to catch the morning light, the corridor that was wide enough for prayer mats and Sunday races.

He wasn't designing from the textbook.

He was designing from the threshold.

The place between what was and what could be.

And as the lines began to connect, Vihaan whispered — almost without knowing:

"Let this house carry the salt of what I left behind."

The common study room smelled like instant noodles, menthol balm, and borrowed ambition.

Desks were pushed into makeshift clusters. Yellow tube lights hummed overhead. Someone had drawn a smiling cockroach on the whiteboard and labeled it "our TA."

Vihaan walked in with his folder tucked under his arm. Nikhil waved him over, mouth full of Maggi, spoon dangling precariously from the cup.

"We're all dying together," he announced. "Might as well draft in company."

Around the table were three other students from Civil: Ramesh from Chennai, who designed bridges in his free time for fun. Ira from Nagpur, who always wore mismatched socks and carried three pens like weapons. And Aaryan, the soft-spoken boy who drank tea like it was therapy.

They were all hunched over their drawings, muttering about line weights and staircase placements.

"Mine looks like a jail," Ira sighed, holding up her sketch. "Straight lines. No light. Very dystopia-core."

"Mine looks like my old apartment," Ramesh said, frowning. "Two balconies. No peace."

"Mine has five windows but no soul," Aaryan added, shrugging.

Vihaan smiled. He didn't speak yet.

Nikhil wiped his hand on his shorts and leaned over his draft dramatically.

"See this?" he pointed. "Living room, center. Three bean bags. One TV. No walls. Total chaos. It's not functional but it's exactly like my nani's house. She ran a beauty parlour out of our kitchen. Clients would walk through while I was brushing my teeth."

Everyone laughed.

"She had this cat," he added, eyes glinting, "named L'Oreal."

Vihaan chuckled.

Then Ira asked, "What about you, Goa boy? What's home to you?"

The table went quiet.

Not expectant. Just... soft.

Vihaan tapped his pencil once against the desk.

"Home?" he repeated. "It's... the sound of jasmine dropping onto tile. A towel that never really dries. A corridor you can race through barefoot. And an old woman who threads silence into flowers."

The room exhaled.

Ramesh nodded slowly. "Damn. That sounds like a poem."

"Or a perfume ad," Nikhil added, tossing a pillow at him. "'Silence by Vihaan — Eau de Aachi.'"

Vihaan laughed — louder than he expected.

And suddenly the room didn't feel borrowed.

It felt shared.

They returned to their drafts, but the tension had melted. Rulers moved smoother. Pens tapped in rhythm. Even the cockroach on the whiteboard seemed less judgmental.

And in the middle of all that the sketching, the slurping, the stories Vihaan felt something shift again.

Not dramatically.

Just a quiet settling. Like furniture that had finally found its corners.

The architecture courtyard was quiet that afternoon too quiet for campus.

A place of columns and overgrown bougainvillaea, it held silence like a museum holds echoes. Vihaan had come for shade, looking for somewhere to revise his second draft away from the crowded hostel.

And there she was again.

Sitting cross-legged on the edge of a sun-warmed bench, sketchbook open on her lap, a black pen dancing like it had its own heartbeat.

The sketching girl.

Same braid. Same quiet intensity.

Her pencil paused as she noticed him not surprised, just vaguely amused.

Vihaan hovered a second too long.

"Still pretending to be invisible?" she asked, eyes not leaving her page.

"Still drawing the world before it notices you," he replied.

She looked up. Smiled. This time, it reached her eyes.

He sat on the other end of the bench, careful not to spill into her space.

"You always sketch buildings?" he asked.

"Mostly," she said, shading the roof of what looked like a temple. "Buildings don't pretend. They're honest in a way people rarely are."

Vihaan nodded. "I'm working on a residential draft for my design class. But I keep slipping into memory."

"That's not a slip," she said. "That's a foundation."

He turned slightly toward her. "But how do you draw a place you don't live in anymore without turning it into a monument?"

She paused.

Then gently, "You don't. You draw it like you're still living there. Even if only in the dust."

He looked at her sketch. It wasn't clean. It wasn't symmetrical. But it breathed.

"Your lines curve," he said.

"They have to," she replied. "Nothing worth remembering was ever built in straight lines."

Vihaan smiled. "I'm Vihaan."

She didn't look up. "I remember."

"You're...?" "Meera."

He let the name sit in the air like a fingerprint.

They didn't say much after that. Just sketched. Side by side. Like two pages in the same book.

As the sun dipped, she closed her book and stood.

Before walking away, she turned slightly, as if deciding something.

"Your walls are too straight," she said.

"Excuse me?"

"In your plan," Meera added. "You're designing to impress. But houses don't impress. They hold. Find the part of you that leans a little and let the walls follow."

And with that, she walked away.

Vihaan sat for a long time after she left, eyes still on the point where her sketchbook had rested.

His draft was technically correct.

But now, it felt... hollow.

He pulled it out. Traced the edges with his fingers.

And slowly, deliberately, began to draw again

This time, with lines that didn't just connect rooms.

But remembered why they were built.

The studio buzzed like a subdued hive paper rustling, pencil strokes, the occasional outburst of laughter muffled by walls that had heard better designs and worse breakdowns.

Vihaan walked in with his draft held flat between two sketchbooks, like a bird he wasn't sure could fly.

He was meeting Anay a fourth-year Civil senior who Nikhil swore by. "He builds better feedback than buildings," he'd said. "Brutal, but honest."

Vihaan found him near the back table, sipping black coffee from a ceramic cup shaped like a cement mixer.

"You're the Goa kid," Anay said, without looking up.

"Vihaan."

Anay extended his hand without enthusiasm. "Let's see it."

Vihaan slid his sheet across the table, feeling suddenly too warm in his own skin.

Anay examined the layout in silence.

The silence stretched.

Stretched longer.

Then finally, a sigh.

"This is neat," he said.

Vihaan relaxed—slightly.

"But it's wrong."

The breath caught in Vihaan's throat.

"It meets the brief," Anay continued. "Everything's where it should be. Rooms align. Light flows. You've used ratios well. Ventilation's solid. But..." He tapped his finger against the common room corner.

"This isn't a house someone lives in. It's a house someone used to live in."

Vihaan said nothing.

Anay leaned forward. "You've designed memory. Not possibility. It's nostalgic. It's safe. But homes don't just hold stories. They invite new ones."

Each word landed like chalk breaking against the board.

"You're still drawing with your back to the future," Anay added, softer now. "Turn around."

Vihaan nodded, stiffly. "Thanks."

Anay sipped his coffee. "Redo it. Not because it's bad. But because you're better than this."

And just like that, the moment ended.

Vihaan stepped out into the hallway, paper rolled tightly in his fist like it had betrayed him.

Outside, the evening was settling over the campus with a golden hush. Boys played cricket in the parking lot. A group laughed near the cycle stand. A sprinkler turned in slow, methodical circles, watering a patch of grass that refused to grow evenly.

He sat on a low wall, elbows on knees, forehead resting on his palms.

It wasn't the critique that hurt.

It was the truth inside it.

He had clung to familiarity.

Turned love into floorplans. But maybe... maybe design wasn't just remembering.

Maybe it was choosing what to make room for.

He stayed there until the sky dimmed, thinking about walls that breathe, windows that welcome, and houses that don't just echo the past but hold the future gently in their arms.

And for the first time, he realized:

He hadn't drawn his house yet.

Only its ghost.

The hostel was mostly asleep.

A few corridors hummed with the last whispers of music, but the world had curled inward, preparing itself for another day. The stars outside blinked without urgency. The fan in Room 17 rotated just enough to sound like it was thinking.

Vihaan sat at his desk.

His earlier draft lay crumpled beside him not discarded in anger, but released, like something that had finished its breath.

He exhaled and laid a fresh sheet on the desk.

And he began.

No ruler yet.

Just pencil.

Free hand.

He didn't start with the walls.

He started with light.

A window, perfectly placed to catch the first breath of dawn.

Then another wider, to hold late afternoons with their sleepy gold. He drew a corridor next not narrow and direct, but curved gently, like memory bending toward laughter.

The living area wasn't at the center this time. It spilled slightly to one side closer to the kitchen. He imagined voices flowing between them, the aroma of something cooking winding its way into conversation.

He paused.

Closed his eyes.

And whispered, "What do I want this house to feel like?"

The pencil moved again.

He widened the doorway.

Added a bench by the entrance.

Not for style but for those small, fidgety moments before leaving: tying shoelaces, finding keys, hugging someone longer than you're supposed to.

He traced a bedroom with a corner built for rain sounds and book pages that curled from dampness.

He drew tiny balconies ones that didn't care about views but were perfect for drying towels and overhearing birds bicker.

He created spaces that waited. Spaces that listened. Spaces that weren't beautiful to look at but felt like exhaling into a favorite t-shirt. And just before finishing, he added something else:

A niche in the hallway a little recessed square.

No purpose.

Just presence.

The kind of place where someone might keep a seashell. Or a folded letter.

Or a pebble from the beach that never really left your pocket.

By the time the lines were complete, the room was quiet in a different way like even the walls were holding their breath.

Vihaan leaned back.

He wasn't sure if it was good.

But he was certain it was true.

This wasn't a home he had lived in.

It was one he was growing into.

And maybe, that was the only blueprint that ever mattered.

The presentation room smelled of ink and tension.

Printed layouts lined the pinboards. Students clustered in corners, adjusting A3 sheets, muttering last-minute justifications. Some had used software to render shadows and texture. Others had labeled everything in all-caps, bold font, bright blue arrows pointing at everything they feared would be ignored.

Vihaan stood near the end of the lineup, his draft rolled gently under his arm, hands tucked into his hoodie like they might disappear.

Dr. Rao walked in — composed, glasses perched low, clipboard in hand like a judge at a silent poetry slam.

"Keep it brief," she said. "Explain what you intended. What you learned. What you'd change. No rehearsed speeches. Speak like you believe it."

One by one, the students stepped forward.

Some spoke with confidence that filled the room. Others read stiffly from their notes. One boy's voice cracked and he pretended it was part of his "creative delivery."

Vihaan's turn came last.

He walked up slowly, heart steady — not still, but not panicked either. He pinned his draft to the board.

No background music. No digital renders.

Just paper. Pencil. Pencil marks that didn't erase perfectly.

He cleared his throat. "This is a house," he began, voice soft but even. "It has two bedrooms, a kitchen, a common area. But more than that... it has light where mornings begin, and space where silence is allowed to sit."

A few heads tilted.

Vihaan continued.

"I started this draft thinking I had to recreate the house I left behind. But that house... was made of memory. This one is made of air, and movement, and the kind of warmth that doesn't have a word."

He pointed to the niche he'd added.

"This part doesn't serve a function. But it reminds. That's enough."

Silence.

Not the awkward kind.

The full kind.

Dr. Rao stepped forward. Adjusted her glasses. Said nothing for a moment longer than comfort allowed.

Then she simply said, "You've stopped drawing rooms. You've started imagining lives."

Vihaan blinked.

That was it.

No applause.

No scores.

Just that sentence and a faint, almost imperceptible nod.

He stepped down.

Heart quiet. Lighter.

Nikhil caught his eye from across the room and mouthed, "Bridges, bro."

Mukund didn't say anything, but tapped the desk once a code Vihaan hadn't learned, but understood.

And as Vihaan rolled his sheet gently, something settled in his chest.

It wasn't pride.

It was placement.

Like he had finally found the shape he was meant to fill.

Not as an engineer.

Not even as a student.

But as someone who knew now: home isn't always something you return to.

Sometimes, it's something you dare to design.

CHAPTER SIX

WHERE THE SEA BEGINS AGAIN

It was the kind of evening that passed unnoticed. Clouds hung like forgotten thoughts above the IIT campus. The wind carried the faintest scent of fried snacks from the canteen. And Vihaan had just returned from a late class, his shoulders tired from more than his backpack.

Room 17 was empty.

Mukund had left a note on the whiteboard: Gone to library. Might become fossil.

Nikhil was out practicing for a hostel cricket match that none of them were taking seriously.

Vihaan dropped his bag, kicked off his sandals, and reached for the water bottle near the window.

That's when he saw it.

A letter.

Propped neatly against his sketchbook, as if it knew where it belonged.

The envelope was the color of faded sunlight, its corners soft with the weight of untold journeys. His name written in his mother's rounded, careful script always a little slanted to the right, always like she was afraid to press too hard.

No stamp. It must've been sent through someone traveling to the city.

He picked it up.

The paper was warm from the sunlight that had touched it.

And it smelled faintly of turmeric, cloves, and the old teakwood cabinet in their prayer room.

His fingers hesitated.

He hadn't received a letter from home since leaving. Calls were quicker. Messages easier. But this... this was slow. And because it was slow, it was serious.

He opened it gently, like waking a memory.

Inside was a single folded page.

No formal greeting. No filler.

Just his mother's handwriting:

>*"Kanna,*
>
>*Aachi hasn't been well the past few days. She had a spell again. The one that makes her forget whether it's morning or evening. She still asks about your towel. She says it smells like salt and sunlight.*
>
>*We haven't told her much, just that you're studying well. But I can see it in her eyes. She's waiting for something. Maybe just your voice.*
>
>*Don't panic. It's not urgent yet. But if you can, call tomorrow after lunch.*
>
>*She's most alert then.*
>
>*Love, Amma"*

That was all.

No tears came.

Not yet.

But something in his chest bent not like it was breaking, but like it was bowing to the wave that was coming.

He folded the letter carefully and placed it inside his sketchbook between the pages that once held structural diagrams, now soft with rain-like memory.

Outside the window, the sun dipped lower, dragging light across the floor like silk unraveling.

And Vihaan sat there, unmoving.

Listening to the silence like it was the only thing that understood what letters can't say.

The lake behind the Civil block was half-forgotten at this hour.

Most students gathered near the mess, or under lit corridors, trading jokes and notes and plans. But Vihaan walked slowly along the muddy path that hugged the lake's curve, the folded letter a silent weight in his pocket.

The air had that scent part rain, part dust, part something older.

A lone dog padded past him, tail wagging without reason. Somewhere behind, the dull echo of a cricket match — appeals, laughter, the hollow thunk of ball on bat.

But in Vihaan's head, everything was hushed.

He thought of Aachi's morning rituals.

The way she circled the puja room three times, muttering prayers under her breath like they were gossip she was too polite to say aloud.

The way she scolded the crows "Why do you shout so early? Even the gods aren't ready yet!" and then fed them anyway, her hand steady with broken rice.

The way she always left one spoonful of every dish in a separate steel katori — for the house spirits, she claimed, "or maybe just for visiting ancestors."

Vihaan smiled faintly at that.

He passed the old banyan tree and sat at the stone bench with cracked corners.

The lake reflected nothing tonight — not stars, not moon, not sky.

Just black water holding the shape of everything it couldn't show.

Aachi had once told him, "Water remembers what you don't."

He hadn't understood it then.

Now he wasn't sure he wanted to.

His hands curled around the edge of the bench.

It wasn't just illness. It was her soul slowly loosening its anchor, like a boat drifting farther with each unseen tide.

And Vihaan didn't know what to do with that kind of goodbye the kind that comes in pieces, like an old wall crumbling where you least expect it.

He closed his eyes.

And for a moment, he could feel her fingers against his forehead, pressing a dot of kumkum.

"Soft is not weak, kanna. Soft is what survives."

The wind shifted.

Leaves rustled like memory being rehearsed.

And Vihaan whispered into the darkness, "Just a little longer, Aachi. Please."

The water didn't reply.

But the silence that followed wasn't empty.

It was holding something.

A presence. A prayer.

And Vihaan stayed not to fix the sadness, but to honour it. Because some silences don't ask for answers; they only ask to be witnessed. The next afternoon, Vihaan skipped lunch.

He told Nikhil he wasn't hungry. He told Mukund he had to revise for a lab. Both lies, softened by how easily they slipped from his mouth.

He walked to the far side of campus, past the computer lab, down a shaded path where the wind always moved sideways, as if looking for someone it had once known.

There, near the edge of the abandoned basketball court, where the reception was strongest, he stood still and dialed home.

One ring.

Two.

"Hello?" His mother's voice, cautious.

"Amma. It's me."

"Vihaan." A pause. Not surprise. Relief.

She didn't ask how he was. She didn't need to.

"Hold on," she said softly. "I'll get her."

A minute passed.

Maybe two.

Each second pulled taut with silence and wind.

Then: a rustle.

Then: a sound — dry, low, like rusted hinges.

"Kanna?"

Aachi.

Vihaan's grip on the phone tightened.

"Aachi," he breathed, unsure what to say next.

Her voice crackled like paper in a flame. "Why is the sea so quiet today?"

Vihaan blinked. "What do you mean?"

"It's not shouting at the shore. It's... waiting. I think it's waiting for you."

The words sliced through him not with pain, but with a soft ache only people who loved you without language could cause.

"I miss you," he said, voice trembling.

There was a silence. Then a sigh like wind leaving the body.

"I made dosas today. But I burned the first one. You weren't here to flip it."

He smiled, even as tears welled in his eyes. "Save me the last one."

"I always do," she whispered.

Then her voice faded.

A shuffle. Another breath.

And his mother came back on the line. Her voice was firm, but her breath betrayed her.

"She has good moments. That was one of them. But they come and go like tide now."

Vihaan nodded into the emptiness.

"I'm sorry," he said.

"You don't have to be," his mother replied. "Just... call again tomorrow."

He promised.

The call ended.

And Vihaan stood there, still holding the phone, like he could press it to his chest and maybe, somehow, the sea would echo back.

Behind him, life continued: students, footsteps, murmurs of lectures and deadlines.

But Vihaan stood outside all of it.

Suspended between what was and what might be taken.

And in the gentle hush of campus afternoon, he whispered again —

"Stay, Aachi. Just until I learn how to carry your name across oceans without breaking."

The sun was low when Vihaan returned to the lake.

Same bench. Same silence. Only the air had changed thicker now, more golden. The kind of evening that held its breath, as if unsure whether to end or stretch forever.

Meera was already there.

Sketchbook in her lap. Hair pulled up in a careless knot that had begun to collapse on one side. She didn't look up as he approached.

Vihaan hesitated.

Then sat.

A few inches of wood between them.

She didn't ask why he was there.

He didn't ask what she was drawing.

They just listened — to birds trading secrets in the trees, to the soft slap of water kissing the bank.

"I called home," he said finally, voice thin.

Meera kept her eyes on her sketch. "Bad news?"

"No." He paused. "Not yet."

Her pencil paused too.

Then moved again.

"My brother used to say that some days don't need full sentences," she said. "Just people who know what the silence means."

Vihaan glanced sideways at her.

Her fingers were still moving slow, steady. She wasn't shading anything in. Just outlining shapes, suggestions, maybe something only she could see.

He wanted to ask.

Didn't.

Instead, he said, "Do you ever feel like you're forgetting them while they're still here?"

Meera nodded once. "Every day."

A breeze picked up, lifting the corner of her page. She pressed it down with her palm.

Vihaan looked at the sketch.

It wasn't a monument she sketched. It was a doorway part hope, part farewell light slipping out like a whispered memory. Light spilling out, but only just.

He didn't ask what it meant.

He didn't need to.

"Sometimes I feel like if I draw the people I miss," she said, "I'll trap them. Make them too still."

Vihaan breathed, slow. "But what if the drawing keeps them alive?"

Meera closed her sketchbook. "That's what I'm afraid of."

The wind shifted again.

They sat in the hush that followed, like children who had wandered too far into a temple and didn't know whether to pray or whisper.

Vihaan picked up a pebble near his foot. Smooth, flat, familiar.

"I didn't know missing someone could start before they leave," he said.

"That's when it's the worst," Meera replied. "When they're still reachable. But already fading."

She stood, dusted off her skirt.

"I hope she stays," she added. "Long enough for you to remember her without guilt."

Vihaan looked up.

Their eyes met for just a second.

Then she walked away, sketchbook tucked under her arm like a secret.

And Vihaan sat there, pebble in hand, wondering whether grief was less about what you lose... ...

and more about what you carry after.

Room 17 was quiet.

The kind of quiet that hung in the corners not heavy, but folded. Like a blanket no one touched all day.

Mukund wasn't there. Nikhil was likely still at the cricket nets. The overhead light buzzed faintly, casting everything in that familiar yellow that made things feel older than they were.

Vihaan dropped his bag.

And went straight to the shelf.

His fingers found it instantly.

The red towel.

Still stiff at the edges, still slightly faded from sea and soap, still warm somehow even in a room that hadn't seen sunlight in hours.

He brought it to his face.

Inhaled.

Salt. Coconut oil. That faint, untraceable smell of summer afternoons back home — when the breeze ran through the house like it was chasing a story and the towel flapped outside like a flag that didn't belong to any nation but theirs.

He sat on his bed.

Held it in his lap.

And let the silence grow.

Not because he wanted to cry.

But because he finally could.

Tears didn't fall like a storm.

They arrived the way Aachi used to quietly, carrying something wrapped in banana leaf, whispering, Eat before it gets cold.

He reached for his journal. The one he never admitted he kept. The one with sketches, ticket stubs, and crumpled bits of lines he never finished writing.

And he wrote.

Today I held a towel and forgot where I was.

Today I breathed like the sea was inside me, not beside me.

Today I missed the way Aachi called my name — not the full word, just the sound at the end, like a wave that knows how to return.

I think love is the smell that stays on things you no longer wear.

I think grief is remembering how to fold something you haven't used in months.

I think I'm scared she'll leave before I say something worth remembering.

And I don't know how to say thank you to a woman who built her life around feeding others and forgot to feed her own memories.

> "*Aachi,*
> *If you're listening:*
> *I'm building something. Slowly. Silently.*
> *And every brick remembers your voice.*"

He closed the book.

Tucked it back into the drawer.

And folded the towel — carefully, like prayer.

Not because he was done missing her.

But because some things you fold when you're not ready to let go...

...and fold again when you finally are.

The first drop landed on his sleeve like punctuation. Vihaan looked up — the clouds hung low, the air thick with that electric quiet that always came before soft rain. Not a storm. Not a warning.

Just a drizzle that felt like the world saying, It's okay to feel too much.

He walked without destination.

Past the Civil block, where chalkboards were being wiped clean for the next morning. Past the mess hall, where spoons clinked against steel like clockwork. Past the banyan tree, where two boys shared a headphone and whispered lyrics neither of them would admit to knowing.

The drizzle grew steadier.

So did the hush inside him.

Raindrops caught on his lashes. On his forearms. In the fold of his shirt.

And somehow, he didn't want to be indoors.

He turned toward the backside of the hostel block — the place where the drain always overflowed, and the wild grass grew tall in protest.

There, under the old tamarind tree, sat Nikhil.

Not shouting.

Not dancing.

Just sitting, arms folded over his knees, hair slick from rain, eyes staring out like he was watching something only he could see.

Vihaan hesitated.

Then joined him.

Neither spoke.

The rain did all the talking — soft taps on leaves, on mud, on memories they hadn't said out loud yet.

After a while, Nikhil broke the silence.

"Your Aachi's sick, isn't she?"

Vihaan blinked.

"How did you—?"

"You've been walking like your backpack weighs more than your body," Nikhil said. "You've barely touched lunch. And your towel's back on the line like it's trying to signal home."

Vihaan let out a short breath. Not quite a laugh. Not quite a sob.

"I'm scared," he said.

Nikhil nodded.

Then looked up at the sky. "My grandfather died two years ago. I was here. Couldn't go home in time. I didn't cry. Not because I didn't care. But because I didn't know how to cry in a place that didn't know him."

The rain picked up slightly — steady, not rushing.

"You don't have to do anything, Vihaan," Nikhil continued. "You just have to stay standing."

"I don't feel like I'm standing."

"That's okay," Nikhil said, "Some days, sitting under a tree in the rain is a win."

A pause.

Then, softer, "She'd be proud of you, you know."

Vihaan didn't answer.

He just watched the water carve little paths in the mud, winding between roots, disappearing into the grass.

The rain eased, leaving the air thick and clean.

And the two boys sat a while longer, in a silence that didn't need translation.

The temple wasn't grand. It was the kind of place that forgot to ask for devotion and was holier for it.

Just a small square room near the mechanical department whitewashed walls, a low ceiling, and two flickering diyas in steel holders that seemed older than the campus itself.

Vihaan hadn't been there before.

He hadn't needed to be.

But that evening, as the sky stretched into navy and the earth smelled like wet stone, his feet moved on their own slow, deliberate, like following a memory he hadn't lived yet.

The door was open.

Inside, the floor was cool, smooth worn by footsteps of those who came not to pray, but to pause. A single brass bell hung from the lintel, gently swaying though no wind touched it.

He stepped inside.

Nobody else was there.

No chants. No flowers. Just silence held gently in four corners.

A small framed photo of Ganesha sat at the far end garlanded with faded marigolds and streaks of ash from old incense sticks. But Vihaan didn't move toward it.

Instead, he walked to the side platform where unlit candles sat in a basket wax twisted into shapes that reminded him of mango leaves and childhood festivals.

He picked one.

Placed it carefully in the corner niche.

Lit the match.

Watched the flame catch hesitantly at first, then with quiet confidence

. He didn't close his eyes.

He just... stood there.

Letting the silence wrap around him like a towel fresh from the sun.

He didn't know what he was asking for.

He didn't even know if he was asking.

But something in him needed this — not as a ritual, but as release.

A soft exhale.

A moment to say:

"I'm here.

I'm holding what hurts.

I won't let it fall."

He placed a jasmine petal beside the candle — one he'd found on the walk there, still fresh from someone else's offering, or maybe the sky.

It wasn't much.

But it was his.

Outside, the wind stirred again.

The brass bell whispered once.

And Vihaan stepped back, nodded once, and turned toward the door.

As he left, he looked over his shoulder.

The flame still danced.

Not like a cry.

Not like a scream.

But like memory saying, "I'm still with you."

CHAPTER SEVEN

LETTERS IN THE LIGHT

The lecture hall was emptying with the usual urgency notebooks snapped shut, bags zipped in unison, and a sea of chairs creaking with the relief of escape. Professor Naresh Kumar had just finished a session on structural mechanics beam behaviors, lateral forces, and the art of load redistribution. Most students left those classes with notebooks heavy with formulas and hearts light with escape.

Vihaan stayed back, as he often did.

Not out of duty.

But because leaving felt like interrupting something unfinished. He was slowly packing his books when the professor's voice reached him.

"Vihaan, right?"

He turned.

Professor Naresh Kumar stood by the edge of the blackboard, wiping his glasses with the end of his sleeve. He was older than most of the department silver hair, eyes like slow rivers, and a voice that always sounded like it had been filtered through quietness.

"Yes, sir," Vihaan replied, standing instinctively straighter.

The professor stepped closer, but not hurriedly. He moved like someone who had long stopped trying to outrun time.

"I saw your submission for the foundation load analysis," he said. "The calculation sheet was... ordinary."

Vihaan blinked. "I'll redo it if"

"But," the professor interrupted, gently, "your annotation caught my eye."

Vihaan frowned.

"You wrote, and I quote," the professor smiled, "'Every structure holds more than its own weight. Sometimes, it holds the doubt of the one building it.'"

Vihaan's ears turned warm.

He'd jotted that on the margin more as a passing thought to himself than anything intended for review.

Professor Kumar continued, "It's rare to find someone who thinks in pressure and poetry."

Vihaan didn't know what to say.

So he nodded.

The professor looked at him for a moment not evaluating, just observing.

"If you're free this evening," he said, "come by my office. "I don't grade curiosity," he said, "but I listen for where it grows."

Vihaan blinked. "You mean... like an appointment?"

"No," the professor said, already turning away. "Just a conversation. About structures. Or the ones we build inside ourselves."

Then he paused at the door.

"My office is at the end of the west corridor. The one with the loose tile. You'll feel it under your feet. Like memory."

And with that, he walked out.

Vihaan stood alone for a few seconds longer than necessary.

Not because he was stunned.

But because someone had seen him.

Not the neat diagrams.

Not the GPA.

But the margin.

And somehow, that felt stronger than any grade he could have gotten. The west corridor was quieter than the rest of campus.

Maybe it was the time of day that post-lunch hush when the sun slanted sideways and the world seemed to breathe slower. Or maybe it was something else. Something about this part of the institute always felt... less rushed. Like it had nothing to prove.

Vihaan walked slowly, his thumb tracing soft circles over the callus on his drawing hand a small scar left by dreaming too much. It wasn't nervousness. Not exactly.

It was weight.

The quiet kind like water in your palm. You didn't realize you were carrying it until you looked down.

He replayed the conversation with Professor Naresh in his head.

The way he had said "pressure and poetry" without even blinking. The way he referenced that scribble on the margin like it was a thesis. The way he had noticed something no TA, no grader, no classmate ever had.

Not what he built, but how he thought about what held it up.

Vihaan glanced up as he passed the row of aging faculty rooms. The windows had dust caught in the edges. A crow dozed on a parapet. Somewhere in the next block, someone practiced tabla the rhythm soft and searching, like a heartbeat testing its own tempo.

At the end of the corridor, the world tilted a little under his foot just enough for memory to slip through.

The tile. Just as Professor Naresh had said a subtle give underfoot. Not a crack. Just... a softness. Like memory pressing back.

He smiled.

It was ridiculous. And quietly perfect.

The door beside it was ajar, a nameplate slightly faded from years of monsoon light:

Prof. N. Kumar – Civil & Environmental Systems

No gold letters. No plaques. Just a brass hook with a ring of wind chimes beside it small, wooden, delicate. They didn't make sound unless the door moved.

Vihaan paused.

Took one deep breath.

And knocked gently.

The chimes stirred. Not fully. Just enough.

A whisper of a welcome.

"Come in," said the voice inside warm, without ceremony.

Vihaan pushed open the door.

And stepped inside, carrying with him not his assignment, not his résumé, not even questions...

...but the quiet hope that maybe, just maybe, being seen could be its own kind of structure.

The first thing Vihaan noticed was the smell old paper, steel files, and something faintly woody, like dried vetiver.

Professor Naresh's office didn't look like it belonged to an engineer.

It looked like it belonged to a collector of forgotten truths.

One side of the room was a wall of books bent at the corners, wedged in sideways, their spines cracked and proud. Some titles read like poetry despite their precision: Foundations and Failures, Earth Retains, Dynamics of Stillness.

Pinned along the adjacent wall were soil classification maps, blackand-white photographs of bridges mid-construction, and a series of hand-drawn sketches showing cross-sections of canals that looked like veins from a body he couldn't name.

At the far end, a small model of a cantilevered balcony sat beside a teacup with a chipped edge.

And amidst it all, at the cluttered desk, sat Professor Naresh — sleeves rolled up, flipping slowly through a yellowing notebook, as if it were a diary more than a lecture note.

He looked up as Vihaan stepped in.

"Close the door," he said gently. "Let's keep the world out, for a moment."

Vihaan obeyed.

The door clicked shut.

And the world... did, in fact, quiet.

Naresh gestured to the chair opposite him. Not stiffly. Not formally. Just a wave of the hand, like he was inviting someone to a late afternoon story.

"You're wondering why I asked you here."

Vihaan nodded, unsure whether to speak yet.

"It's not for correction," the professor said. "Or evaluation. You're not in trouble."

A smile flickered at the edge of his voice.

"I saw something in your thought process. Not just the math — though your math is fine. I saw someone who doesn't just want to build things..."

He paused. "

...but someone who wants to understand why things hold up at all." Vihaan felt his throat tighten a little. In a good way. Like he'd been handed something fragile and warm.

Naresh leaned back in his chair, hands folding gently over his stomach.

"Tell me," he asked, "what's the first thing you notice when you walk into a building?"

Vihaan blinked. "Most people say light. Or layout. Or symmetry."

The professor nodded. "And you?"

Vihaan thought for a second.

Then: "I notice where the dust settles. And where it doesn't."

Naresh smiled — full and genuine now. "Exactly."

They didn't speak for a moment.

The wind outside stirred the chimes again.

And Vihaan realized: this wasn't going to be a lecture.

It was going to be an unfolding.

Professor Naresh poured the tea from a wide ceramic kettle, its crack sealed not with repair, but with remembering. Vihaan noticed the line immediately.

"Civil engineers," Naresh said, "should know better than to discard something because of one fault line."

Vihaan smiled. "Kintsugi for infrastructure?"

"Precisely," the professor nodded, handing over a chipped cup. "Though don't suggest it for flyovers."

The tea was warm, slightly over-steeped, scented faintly with lemongrass and ginger. It didn't taste like hostel chai — this one lingered in the mouth, earthy and slow.

They sat in silence for a few moments, the kind that didn't rush to be filled.

Then Naresh spoke. "You know, the more I teach this subject, the more I think about foundations as personalities."

Vihaan raised an eyebrow.

"How so?"

Naresh sipped slowly. "Some are shallow. Fast to pour. Easy to cure. Cheap. And just like that — you can build over them in no time."

A pause.

"But some... are deep. Quiet. Unimpressive at first. They take longer. Ask more of you. And no one sees them once they're done. But they hold. They last."

Vihaan set his cup down, his fingers tapping the rim thoughtfully.

"I don't know which one I am yet," he said, after a pause.

"Don't rush to be a high-rise," Naresh replied. "Even bungalows remember better."

Vihaan let out a soft laugh.

Then asked, "Do you ever think we're just trying to build permanence in a world that keeps shifting?"

Naresh's eyes twinkled.

"That," he said, "is the paradox of civil engineering, Vihaan. You learn how to resist movement. But you live by learning how to move with it."

The window creaked as a gust of wind pushed through the frame, lifting one page from the professor's desk — an old site plan, annotated in red ink and fingerprints.

"Most students," Naresh continued, "focus on load-bearing calculations. Flexural strength. Shear resistance. All necessary. But rarely do they ask: what lives in the space we make? What breathes there? Who waits for what to arrive?"

Vihaan stared at the model on the table again — the cantilevered balcony that seemed to defy logic.

"Did you build that?" he asked.

Naresh smiled. "A student did. Ten years ago. Failed every test. But gave me that on the last day. Said it was how she saw her future — unsupported, but reaching."

Vihaan didn't speak.

He didn't need to.

Because somehow, the tea had told him more than any formula could:

That maybe what mattered wasn't just what you held up...

But how you made space for what might one day stand there, too.

Professor Naresh stood slowly, moving toward the old cabinet in the corner not the one filled with textbooks and journals, but the smaller wooden one, its hinges creaking like it remembered too much.

He pulled open the bottom drawer.

Inside, stacked like sediment, were dozens of student sketchbooks and project logs some bound in leather, others tied with string, one wrapped in what looked like an old dhoti.

Vihaan leaned in as the scent of old ink and musty paper rose time made tangible.

"These are my favorites," Naresh said. "Not the toppers. Not the polished ones. These are the ones where people tried, hesitated, scratched, rewrote... and left a part of themselves."

He pulled out a few and set them gently on the table.

"Pick one," he said. "You'll know which."

Vihaan hesitated, then reached for a slim book with a frayed cloth spine. No name on the cover. Just a faint blue thread hanging loose, like it had been tugged by time.

He opened it.

The first few pages were calculations — messy, revised, coffeestained. Then a loose sheet slipped out.

A sketch.

Hand-drawn, uneven, edges curled.

Not of a building.

Not a bridge.

But of a single staircase — spiraling downward. Each step labeled not with measurements, but with thoughts:

"This is where I paused."

"This is where I almost quit."

"This is where my teacher said, try again."

"This is where I began."

Vihaan stared at it. Not because it was technically remarkable — it wasn't.

But because it felt... true.

Like someone had drawn not to impress, but to remember.

"Who did this?" he asked quietly.

Naresh didn't answer immediately.

He leaned against the desk and sipped the last of his tea.

"She dropped out in the third year. Family issues. I still think she would've made one of the best structural analysts in this country."

Vihaan's chest tightened.

Not in pity.

But in recognition.

Because that sketch wasn't just a design.

It was a map.

And for a moment, he saw his own staircase too — invisible, but echoing hers.

With pauses.

And almost-quits.

And words that pulled him forward.

"Can I...?" Vihaan began.

Naresh smiled. "Take a photo. Keep it. Sometimes, the things that don't make it to the final draft are the ones that make us who we are."

Vihaan did.

Gently.

And as he looked at it one last time, he whispered, "This isn't about building tall, is it?"

Naresh shook his head.

"It's about building deep. And knowing which cracks are worth sealing and which are meant to stay."

Vihaan gathered his things slowly.

Not out of reluctance, but reverence like packing up after a story that left the air a little warmer.

He tucked his notebook under one arm, the teacup already washed and returned without being asked. The room felt different now not because it had changed, but because he had. The shelves looked less like archives and more like conversation starters. The chimes, softer now, seemed to pulse with something known.

He turned toward Professor Naresh, who was gently brushing the table clear of the dust left by old folders.

"Thank you," Vihaan said, his voice even, but not rehearsed. "For... all of this."

Naresh didn't nod. He simply looked up.

"There's nothing to thank me for. You're the one who brought the questions."

Vihaan smiled. "I didn't even know I had them."

"You did," Naresh said. "You just hadn't built the structure to hear them echo yet."

Vihaan opened the door halfway.

Paused.

And then, Naresh spoke again — not louder, just... more true.

"You know," he said, "you have the hands of someone who'll never build just what the world demands."

Vihaan turned back slightly. "Is that a compliment or a warning?"

Naresh smiled. "Yes."

Vihaan laughed that soft, surprised kind of laugh that slips out before you can hide it.

And then the professor added, as if offhand:

"Don't rush to become impressive, Vihaan. Just become felt."

It landed like a nail through silence.

Not pain.

Placement.

Something to hold the moment together.

Vihaan didn't respond right away. He couldn't.

So he did what he had learned to do best in the last few months:

He carried it.

Folded the sentence like a note in his chest pocket.

Let it rest against the beat of everything he was still figuring out.

And with one final look at the chimes, at the cracked teacup, at the man who had just offered a version of home inside a faculty room —

Vihaan stepped out.

The door clicked gently behind him.

But something had opened.

And it would not close again.

The campus had begun to change its face.

The lamps along the walkways blinked on one by one hesitant at first, then steady, casting golden halos on the wet cobblestones. Trees whispered in the evening breeze. Somewhere in the distance, a group of students laughed mid-sprint, chasing a frisbee like it meant something sacred.

Vihaan walked without urgency.

He didn't check his phone.

Didn't play music.

He just let his steps find their rhythm soft, certain, unhurried. The corridor behind him still echoed with the professor's words: Don't rush to become impressive. Just become felt.

What did that even mean?

Vihaan wasn't sure yet.

But he knew it felt different than praise. It wasn't about doing well. It was about doing true.

He passed the cricket field, where Nikhil threw himself onto the mud like joy didn't mind getting dirty. A few hostel mates waved. One yelled, "Dinner, da!" but Vihaan just raised a hand in return and kept walking.

His thoughts weren't heavy.

They were quiet.

And in that quiet, new questions began to stir:

What if structures weren't just answers, but invitations?

What if foundations didn't only carry load, but carried stories?

What if you could build a future that remembered the weight of what made you gentle?

He reached the footbridge that crossed the central pond where dragonflies skimmed like punctuation across still water. The wind picked up, brushing past his shirt like a sentence in a language he almost understood.

He paused in the middle of the bridge.

Looked down.

And for a moment, he saw his reflection — blurred, tilted, touched by leaves floating in the water.

Not clear.

But real.

And that was enough.

He reached into his sketchbook and scribbled a single line across the margin of a class note:

Today I wasn't graded.

But I was heard.

And that might be stronger than steel.

The page fluttered in the breeze as he closed the book.

He exhaled not from exhaustion, but from arrival.

And walked on.

Not toward a destination.

But into something opening.

CHAPTER EIGHT

THE WEIGHT OF SMALL THINGS

The fan clicked faintly as it rotated, blades slicing the silence into quarters. Room 17 was still except for the slow, rhythmic breath of Mukund on the top bunk.

Vihaan had woken early.

Not by alarm. Not by sunlight.

But by something softer. A sound that didn't quite fit the quiet.

It was Mukund.

Mumbling.

Vihaan remained still, eyes open in the half-dark, the grey morning light slipping through the slit in the curtain.

At first, he thought Mukund was muttering another one of his nighttime rants about load-shedding or unit tests.

But then he heard it again, clearer this time.

"Amma... don't forget my towel..."

The words were soft. Childlike.

Not humorous.

Just... real.

A pause. Then another whisper.

"Where's the rice water, Ma? My stomach hurts again."

Vihaan didn't move.

Didn't dare to.

Because this wasn't a performance. This was the voice of someone far from home, speaking to someone who wasn't there.

A soft ache rose in Vihaan's throat.

Not pity.

Recognition.

We're all carrying things, he thought. Some we mention. Some we sleep with.

Mukund stirred, turned over, and the murmuring stopped.

Vihaan let out a breath.

Sat up slowly.

The light outside had brightened slightly the kind of pale gold that touched the window grills but hadn't yet dared to reach the floor.

He pulled on his hoodie and walked to the small washbasin down the hall. The water sputtered twice before flowing, cold and clear.

As he splashed it over his face, he caught his own reflection hair flattened to one side, eyes still laced with last night's thoughts.

But behind his own face, he saw something else:

Roommates aren't just the ones we share walls with.

They are the ones whose griefs drift down to us in sleep, whose silences we fold around our own breathing without even noticing, whose silences we walk around, whose tired dreams drift down from the top bunk like prayers left unsaid.

Back in the room, Mukund snored once sharply then shifted again. Vihaan didn't mention what he'd heard.

He never would.

But he made a quiet promise to himself:

The next time Mukund talked about his mother's rasam, or complained about how the hostel sambar had "no soul," he'd listen.

Really listen.

Because sometimes, the things that seem small...

...are the things that tell you who someone is when they think no one is watching.

The mess hall buzzed with morning rituals.

Plates clattered. Ladles slapped stainless-steel serving trays. Someone shouted over a missing ID card while another argued over the last slice of bread. The usual chaos — but somehow, Vihaan had stopped finding it abrasive.

He sat at the far end of the second table from the window, where the sunlight slanted just right to catch the steam rising from idlis like halos.

Nikhil plopped down beside him, hair wet, a towel slung around his neck like a prizefighter.

"You look like you fought with your own bucket," Vihaan muttered, tearing a corner of dosa.

"I did," Nikhil said, grinning. "Bucket won."

Across the table, Mukund arrived, already mid-rant.

"Why does the pongal here taste like it's recovering from a breakup?"

Laughter broke out.

Vihaan didn't say anything at first. But then, between bites, he said, almost to himself, "Because it's clinging, but no longer warm."

The table went quiet for a second.

Then Nikhil burst out laughing. "Dude. That's... painfully accurate."

Someone two chairs down leaned in. "What did he say?"

Mukund repeated the line dramatically. More laughter.

Vihaan blinked. "I didn't mean it as a joke."

"That's why it worked," Nikhil said, elbowing him. "You speak in metaphors even when you're just describing breakfast trauma."

Vihaan smirked, hiding it behind a sip of hot sambar.

The conversation turned to an upcoming quiz, to a guy who apparently slept through a viva, to someone's attempt at baking in a rice cooker.

But Vihaan felt it.

That small shift.

That weightless tug of belonging.

Not because he'd tried to be liked.

But because he'd simply been himself.

Someone passed him an extra vada without asking.

Someone else nudged a bottle of water toward his side of the table. These were the invisible stitches that held friendships together the ones you never remembered making, but never forgot feeling. He thought of the ties in a reinforced beam the hidden steel that doesn't carry the full load, but keeps everything from cracking apart.

This moment?

It was one of those ties.

Small.

Silent.

But strong.

It started like any other class.

The lab was too cold the AC always set like someone was refrigerating nervousness. The professor scribbled slab reinforcement diagrams on the board with a kind of artistic rage. Chalk dust hung in the air like consequence.

Vihaan had taken his usual notes detailed, methodical but with his own quiet habits still intact. A bracketed metaphor here. A random observation tucked between formulas there.

It helped him remember.

It made the world feel less... square.

After class, Meera approached him at the hallway's bend — where sunlight always filtered in through the dusty glass, staining the floor with geometric comfort.

"Can I borrow your notes for a day?" she asked. "I zoned out somewhere between deflection and despair."

Vihaan handed them over without hesitation.

"Your handwriting's nicer anyway," she added, already flipping through.

He didn't say it, but the moment she took the book, his chest felt oddly... light.

The notebook returned to him the next morning.

Meera placed it on his desk in class without a word, just a small nod and the hint of a smile like handing back a borrowed sweater that had kept her warm.

Later that evening, alone in Room 17, Vihaan flipped through the pages.

There, on a page filled with moment and shear calculations, he spotted it.

His margin note a single line he barely remembered writing:

Every structure needs a pause. Otherwise, it forgets to breathe.

And just below it, in smaller, neater handwriting, Meera had written:

Some pauses are doorways.

Vihaan stared at it for a long time.

He read it once.

Twice.

Then closed the book slowly, hands still on the cover as if to hold it in place not just physically, but emotionally.

It wasn't flirtation.

It wasn't a grand gesture.

It was recognition.

She hadn't just read the margin she had answered its silence, like a door creaking open in a forgotten house. Not with a smiley face. Not with praise.

But with a thought.

A doorway.

He didn't know what it meant yet.

But suddenly, the line between structural analysis and emotional understanding blurred just enough to let something unexpected in.

And Vihaan smiled — not wide, not obvious.

Just enough to shift the structure of his evening.

It was supposed to be a routine tutorial.

Twelve students, one overstretched TA, and a problem set that looked deceptively simple something about foundation types and differential settlement. Concrete pads versus pile foundations. Load distribution in non-uniform soils.

Most students scribbled answers with mild panic. Some guessed. A few whispered wildly wrong things to one another.

And then there was Arjun — frowning hard at his graph paper, chewing the end of his pen like it owed him an explanation.

Vihaan sat beside him, sketching quietly, not really planning to talk.

Until Arjun muttered, "How can the left side of this house sink and the right stay fine? Isn't that, like, engineering blasphemy?"

Vihaan chuckled under his breath.

"It's actually more common than you'd think."

Arjun looked up.

"You've seen this?"

Vihaan hesitated.

Then said, "We had a beach hut near our village — run by a fisherman named Gopi anna. The hut had four bamboo poles. Every monsoon, two would sink, and he'd prop the floor up with coconut shells."

That got a few people's attention.

Vihaan kept going.

"He didn't understand soil mechanics. But he knew his floor had mood swings."

A small laugh.

Even the TA looked up.

Vihaan reached for a fresh sheet of paper.

"Think of it this way," he said, drawing quickly. "If your foundation rests on coastal clay on one side and rocky fill on the other, rainfall doesn't soak both equally. Clay expands, shifts. The rock? Stays firm."

He sketched a lopsided rectangle — the hut mid-tilt.

"You don't notice it right away. It starts with a door that doesn't close right. Then a stool that wobbles. Then one day, you drop your phone and it rolls away like it has a plan."

More laughter.

But now, they were watching.

And understanding.

Vihaan circled the base of the sketch.

"This is why we learn about differential settlement — not for exams, but because someone's kitchen sink might slide across the floor one day."

The TA raised an eyebrow, amused.

"That was... unusually effective," he said.

Vihaan shrugged. "I think better in beach metaphors."

Arjun grinned. "Man, that actually helped."

And in that moment not loud, not grand Vihaan felt something click inside.

Not ego.

Not brilliance.

Just this quiet truth:

The world he came from had lessons, too. And maybe, just maybe, the way he saw things not in formulas, but in stories was a kind of strength.

The rooftop wasn't meant to be beautiful.

It was uneven. Cracked in places. The water tank stood like a forgotten sentinel in one corner, and an old plastic chair had sunk one leg into the cement permanently, as if giving up.

But at night, with the lights of the city flickering in the distance and stars just barely visible above the smog, it became something else.

A shelter for the unspoken.

Nikhil had dragged Vihaan up there after dinner with a packet of Kurkure and a half-finished bottle of Mazza.

"Come," he said, waving dramatically. "Let us escape from mess food and mid-sem doubt."

They sat on the ledge, feet dangling, Kurkure crackling between them.

"You ever think the moon looks like it's judging us?" Nikhil asked, squinting up.

Vihaan followed his gaze. "Maybe it's just reflecting all our insecurities."

"That's deep, bro," Nikhil said, mock-offended. "Don't bring poetry to a snack fight."

Vihaan grinned, popping a piece in his mouth.

They talked nonsense for a while cricket scores, hostel rumors, which professor might be a secret poet.

Then Nikhil went quiet.

It wasn't abrupt.

Just... a shift in energy.

He leaned back on his palms, staring up.

"I don't think I'm cut out for this," he said suddenly.

Vihaan turned slightly. "For what?"

Nikhil shrugged. "I don't know. All of it. IIT. Pressure. Expectations. My family keeps saying, 'You're the smart one, Nikhil. The achiever.' And I'm just sitting here wondering if I'm going to fail the next fluid mechanics quiz."

Vihaan didn't interrupt.

Didn't rush in with comfort.

He just listened.

Because he knew sometimes what you need isn't reassurance.

It's space to say the scary thing out loud.

"I bombed the last two assignments," Nikhil continued. "Didn't tell anyone. Not even Mukund. Everyone thinks I'm the guy who doesn't care. But I care so much, it keeps me awake."

Vihaan nodded slowly.

"You know what they don't tell you about strong foundations?" he said. "Sometimes the strongest foundations crack where no one looks and that's how they survive, too."

Nikhil looked at him.

"Yeah?"

Vihaan nodded. "And that doesn't mean they're weak. It just means they've been holding a lot."

They sat in silence for a while, the kind that felt stitched together by understanding.

The breeze picked up, tugging lightly at their shirts. Below them, the hostel lights flickered like quiet pulsebeats.

"You think we'll make it?" Nikhil asked.

Vihaan didn't answer right away.

Then, softly: "I think we'll hold."

The notification blinked up just as Vihaan reached the stairwell a single line of digital ink that stopped him in his tracks:

Missed Call – Amma (3 min ago)

His chest tightened.

The kind of tightness that knew what it meant to receive bad news in silence.

His mind moved faster than his feet.

Aachi?

What if something happened again?

Why didn't she message?

He stepped aside, heartbeat thudding.

Dialed back instantly.

One ring.

Two.

Then her voice.

"Vihaan?"

It sounded normal. Not strained. Not panicked.

"Amma. I saw your call. Is everything okay?"

A pause.

Then a small laugh. "Why are you breathing like you ran across the whole station?"

"I—" he exhaled. "Just... saw the call."

Another pause. Then softer.

"Kanna, not every call is a storm. Sometimes a mother just wants to hear her son's voice."

He closed his eyes. Let his body lean against the cool wall beside the staircase.

The relief was sudden and slow, like finding breath after swimming too far from shore.

"I was just packing pickles," she continued. "For the parcel. Wanted to ask if you still like the lemon one or if you've become fancy in Bombay."

Vihaan smiled.

"Lemon. Always lemon."

"And you ate lunch?"

"Yeah. Aloo Paratha."

She made a noise only mothers can make — somewhere between disappointment and disbelief.

"You know that's rice pretending to be food, right?"

He laughed.

The sound surprised him.

It had been a while since laughter had come out without being filtered.

They talked for another minute nothing urgent. Just rice. And socks. And whether the towel he took was still holding up.

Then she said, "Okay. Go. Don't let me interrupt your studies."

"You didn't," Vihaan replied. "You... slowed it down. In a good way."

She hummed.

Then, just before hanging up, she added:

"Tell the sea I said hello."

And she hung up.

Vihaan stood there for a moment, the stairwell quiet except for the occasional echo of footsteps above.

He looked at his phone again.

The screen now blank.

But his chest... not so tight anymore.

Sometimes, he thought, the calls that don't come in emergencies...

...are the ones that remind you you're still part of someone's daily world.

And in that moment, he felt it:

Love wasn't always thunder.

Sometimes it was just a ring.

And someone waiting on the other end with pickles and a memory.

Later that evening, when the heat had thinned into breeze and the shadows leaned longer across campus paths, Vihaan wandered back to the old banyan tree near the admin block.

It wasn't planned.

But something about the day Mukund's sleep-talking, Nikhil's rooftop confession, his mother's soft call had left him... full. Not overwhelmed. Just filled in that quiet, aching way that only simple things can do.

The banyan welcomed him like it always did arms wide, roots trailing like threads in a family sari. He sat at its base, back against the trunk, notebook resting on his knee.

Beside him: a small packet of homemade murukku, the kind tied at the ends with green thread, slightly crushed from travel. His mother had sent it last week. He hadn't opened it until now.

He picked one. Took a bite.

Crunchy. Spicy. And suddenly, memory.

The taste of Sunday afternoons on the porch. Aachi arguing with the crows. Amma humming over boiling oil. His towel drying above the line, swaying as if it, too, was listening.

He closed his eyes.

And that's when he heard the footsteps.

Soft.

Certain.

He opened his eyes to find Meera standing a few feet away sketchbook in one hand, sleeves rolled up to her elbows, wind in her hair like it belonged there.

They didn't speak.

She tilted her head slightly, asking a silent question.

Vihaan gestured to the spot beside him.

She sat.

No ceremony.

No "hello."

Just shared shade.

A few seconds passed.

Then he reached into the packet.

Held it between them.

Didn't say a word.

She looked at it.

Then at him.

Took one.

Ate.

Nodded.

Nothing more.

And somehow, it was everything.

Because there are moments in life that don't need explanation they just need to be. Like a good foundation that doesn't show, or a structure that doesn't creak even when the wind changes direction.

The sun dipped lower.

Their shoulders not touching, but close enough to feel the heat radiate between silences.

Vihaan didn't write anything in his notebook that evening.

But if he had, it would've been this:

Sometimes you don't fall in love in a sentence.

Sometimes, it begins with shared shade and a handful of spice.

And a girl who eats your murukku without asking if it's okay to stay.

SOMETHING THAT HOLDS

The classroom air was heavy with the scent of dust, old books, and slightly overcooked sambhar from the mess hall wafting in through open windows.

Vihaan sat near the side wall his usual seat half-listening, halfsketching a stray thought in the corner of his notebook. A cluster of jagged lines became a slope. Then a retaining wall. Then, unconsciously, a shack he hadn't seen since last monsoon.

"Alright, settle down," came the voice from the front clear, firm, but without edge.

It was Professor Indira, one of the few faculty members who didn't need volume to command attention. Her presence alone felt like standing under a roof supported by the clean geometry of reason.

"We're piloting something new," she began, adjusting her dupatta as she clicked to the next slide. "A short-term design application project. Interdisciplinary where possible. You'll form teams of four. Objective: propose and model a real-world small-scale civil structure. Low-cost, context-sensitive, and ideally... meaningful."

A murmur ran through the class.

She continued, "Bridges. Rainwater harvesting units. Footpaths on slopes. Retaining walls. Tank supports. You'll select your own problem statement. One week to conceptualize. One week to model. One week to refine. Final review by a panel."

Someone at the back raised a hand. "Is this for marks?"

"No," Indira said, smiling faintly. "But if you do it right, it might be for memory."

The line hit Vihaan harder than he expected.

He sat up slightly.

The slide changed again. Sample projects from past years: a bambooframe footbridge in a Tamil Nadu village. A sanitation block for a rural school. A bus shelter with runoff harvesting in Himachal.

Not flashy.

But real.

The kind of structures his village always needed, always patched up, always built with borrowed hope and bent nails.

Vihaan felt something shift in his chest not a spark. More like a pressure point finally being touched.

Professor Indira looked around the room.

"I'm not looking for brilliance," she said. "I'm looking for thinking that holds. Structures that remember their people."

Vihaan's pencil had stopped moving.

Because suddenly, the sketch on the corner of his page didn't feel accidental.

It felt like a beginning.

The classroom emptied slowly not with the usual clamor, but with a kind of deliberate shuffling. No one wanted to look too eager. And yet everyone knew this was the kind of project that would be remembered.

By the time Vihaan had packed his things, most clusters had already begun to form.

Three.

Four.

Three again.

He lingered near the side wall, watching people lean across desks, claim teammates like childhood friends forming cricket teams.

Nikhil spotted him first.

"Oi! You're not going to slink off into some introvert cave, da. Come." Vihaan hesitated.

Then walked over.

Meera was already seated sketchbook closed but her gaze alert, tracking groupings like an observer of weather systems.

Beside her, a lanky boy with glasses and an engineer's frown tapped his pen against his notebook like it owed him clarity.

"This is Aayush," Nikhil said. "My lab partner in geotech. Doesn't talk much. But neither do you. So, poetic symmetry."

Aayush nodded once. No smile. Just quiet acknowledgment.

Vihaan hovered.

Meera looked up at him and, without saying a word, nudged her notebook across the desk making space.

The notebook nudged across the desk wasn't just an invitation. It was a bridge quiet, steady, waiting for him to cross.

A brief silence.

Then Nikhil leaned forward like a football coach at halftime.

"Okay. So. No one here knows what the hell we're doing, but we're all too stubborn to admit it. Which means: we're officially a team."

Meera smiled faintly.

Aayush finally spoke, his voice low but clear.

"We need to start by picking a location or a real-world constraint. That'll shape everything structure, materials, budget."

Vihaan nodded.

But said nothing yet.

Because a thought had already started forming in his mind something half-seen, built not from diagrams but from childhood.

The little bridge over the estuary near his village.

Made of rotting planks, three concrete piers, and the prayers of everyone who crossed it barefoot after sunset.

It had held for decades.

And it had remembered the people who built it.

He didn't share the idea yet.

But he looked at the three people across the desk Nikhil's grin, Meera's unreadable gaze, Aayush's steady focus and thought:

Maybe this is a structure worth being part of.

And maybe this time, he wouldn't just be the boy who sketched in margins.

Maybe this time, he'd be one of the builders.

They met after dinner, huddled around a corner table in the campus library annex the kind of place where whispers sound louder than intentions, and ideas either collapse or take flight.

Nikhil arrived with an unnecessary number of pens. Meera came with two folded maps and a look that said she'd already done her research. Aayush opened his laptop before even sitting.

Vihaan came with his sketchbook.

"Okay," Nikhil said, leaning forward, "who's going to throw the first stone into this theoretical pond?"

Aayush spoke first precise and pointed.

"Rainwater harvesting structure. Urban slum. Bamboo framing. Easy to source. Minimal curing."

Meera raised a brow. "Maybe. But we'll need direct access to a settlement if we want actual community data."

They went back and forth — a little stiff, a little too academic.

Vihaan listened.

Watched.

Waited.

And then, softly: "What about a bridge?"

Three heads turned.

He wasn't used to that much attention. He cleared his throat, thumb grazing the spiral edge of his sketchpad.

"Back home," Vihaan said softly, "there's a narrow slice of water that divides the land like a secret. We built a bridge across it not with blueprints, but with belief." The bridge that crosses it; it's been patched together a hundred times. Planks, stones, rope, even rusted pipes. But it still holds. People carry fish baskets over it. Kids run barefoot across it. And every monsoon, it sinks a little more."

He looked up.

"I'm not saying we build that exact thing. But what if we studied small-span, low-cost pedestrian bridges? Something coastal communities can build using mixed materials reclaimed concrete, local timber. Something that remembers the rhythm of the place it's in."

No one spoke immediately.

Then Meera asked, "What's the load capacity of that bridge?"

Vihaan smiled faintly. "Somewhere between hope and habit."

A soft chuckle from Nikhil.

Aayush, after a beat: "We'll need proper feasibility data. But... it's not a bad prompt."

Vihaan relaxed just slightly.

Meera opened her map again. "There's a village about forty kilometers south of here. Brackish water inlet. I think it's similar. Might even be better for modeling."

Vihaan met her eyes.

She nodded once in that way of hers that said I hear you. And for the first time in the session, he felt something land.

Not an idea.

Not a plan.

A permission.

To contribute.

To belong.

To build something that held where he came from.

The auto ride was bumpy, chaotic, and too loud.

Vihaan sat wedged between Nikhil and a steel survey pole, watching the city thin into uneven pavements, patched roads, and then... something else.

Homes stitched together from tarpaulin and tin, dreams patched between cracked bricks. Sloped drains that tried and failed to contain yesterday's rain. The kind of place the city pretended not to see where every structure was a compromise, and every family a blueprint of improvisation.

The auto pulled into a dusty clearing, stopping near a narrow alley.

"This is the edge of Sector G," Meera said, checking the site map. "The NGO liaison said we could walk around. No photos. Just notes." The group stepped out, adjusting their shoes, backpacks, expectations.

Vihaan followed.

The alleys were barely wide enough for two people. Clotheslines draped above them like bunting. The ground was uneven, shifting between loose bricks and wet patches. A girl in a pink school uniform jumped over a crack that revealed a sewer beneath.

Vihaan slowed near a small concrete slab that passed as a footbridge it tilted downward into a slope. Its joints had eroded, but someone had wedged bricks under one side to level it.

"It's like someone tried to prop up the earth," he whispered.

Nikhil came beside him. "Engineers of necessity, man."

A woman walked past carrying a steel pot of water, balancing it on her hip, bare feet splashing through muddy run-off. She smiled at Meera. Nodded. Kept going.

Vihaan watched the buildings around them if you could call them that. One had a sheet-metal roof held in place by four bricks. Another leaned slightly inward, as though trying to stay upright by whispering to its neighbor.

No rebar.

No symmetry.

But still... they stood.

He paused near a wall made of cement bags flattened and layered between brick rows. There was a child's handprint in the plaster small, deliberate.

It broke something inside him.

"This isn't just about building," he said quietly, almost to himself. "It's about surviving. About holding onto space."

Meera heard him.

She didn't reply. Just walked a little closer.

By the time they reached the main road again, Vihaan's notebook had three sketches, a dozen annotations, and something he hadn't written down yet:

A feeling.

That this — this — is what he wanted to work for.

Not drawings on a board.

But structures that knew the people they held.

The tea stall was barely more than a cart with two plastic stools and a plywood bench wedged between a banyan tree and a faded poster of a political candidate who'd long lost.

But it smelled like home.

Boiling ginger. Melted sugar. Cardamom. Rusted steel.

They ordered three cutting chais and a soda for Aayush, who didn't drink tea "on principle" a fact no one questioned.

Vihaan sat on the end of the bench, arms resting on his knees. His fingers twitched for something to hold. He pulled a pen from his pocket and grabbed a clean tissue from the chipped metal stand.

The others talked beside him about how to frame their feasibility analysis, whether pre-cast concrete would meet the brief, the way the water pooled under one particular house.

Vihaan didn't speak.

He drew.

It started with the estuary near his village.

Two piers.

Rope railing.

A deck slightly curved not by design, but by erosion.

He sketched the small stubbornnesses bricks wedged under tilts, ropes knotted against logic, footsteps trusting planks that no engineer had signed off on they'd seen this morning half bricks under a tilt, one end anchored in a tree root. A line of human movement sketched as silhouettes: a girl with a schoolbag, a man with a sack of rice, a woman carrying water.

And over it all, he drew the lightest curve not structural. Just... suggestion. The arc of balance.

He didn't even realize the others had gone quiet.

"Did you just do that?" Meera asked softly.

Vihaan looked up, surprised.

She leaned closer. "That's... something."

Aayush reached over, tilted the tissue slightly. "Is that the angle from the slope we saw near the inlet?"

Vihaan nodded. "It's not exact. Just a feeling. A thought. Of how it could work."

Nikhil whistled. "Bro. You're wasting your life in lectures. This belongs on a wall."

Vihaan flushed.

"It's not a plan. Just a sketch."

Meera smiled not wide, but real.

"Sometimes sketches are the plan. The rest is just proving them right."

They passed the tissue around carefully, as though it held something fragile.

Because it did.

Not just an idea.

But the moment it became theirs.

Back in the library annex the next evening, the table felt tighter.

Not physically just tenser.

They'd laid out their notes, diagrams, field data, and Vihaan's tissue sketch (now flattened inside a clear folder like a pressed leaf). The project was beginning to take shape and with it, disagreements.

Aayush tapped his pen against the page. "This bridge design while poetic won't survive the first mid-June flood. The slope grading is inconsistent. And we're not accounting for silt drag in the inlet flow."

Nikhil raised an eyebrow. "Dude, we're not building the Golden Gate. It's a community-access bridge."

"But that doesn't mean it can be structurally naive," Aayush shot back. "We're engineers, not storytellers."

There was a pause.

Meera looked at Vihaan.

He hadn't said anything yet.

He was staring at the sketch.

At the pencil lines that didn't argue they just suggested.

Then he spoke not loudly, not defensively. Just enough.

"I'm not asking us to build sentiment," Vihaan said. "I'm asking us to remember who it's for."

Aayush looked up.

"The slope issue is valid," Vihaan continued. "So let's test it. Let's adapt. Raise the central beam support. Angle the footings differently.

But don't dismiss the sketch because it started with a memory."

A beat.

Then: "Memory is a load-bearing wall," Vihaan said. "Structures survive when they remember who they're carrying."

Aayush blinked.

And something in the room shifted not in sound, but in temperature.

Because Vihaan hadn't pushed back to win.

He'd spoken to hold.

And in doing so, he'd given the idea roots.

Meera folded her arms, looking at the sketch again.

"If we do it your way," she said to Aayush, "we get a safe bridge."

She turned to Vihaan.

"If we do it your way, we get a remembered one."

Nikhil grinned. "Let's build the kind that leaves both dry feet and stories."

Aayush said nothing for a moment.

Then, slowly, he nodded.

"I'll recalculate the supports tonight."

Vihaan exhaled.

Not from relief.

But from arrival.

Because for the first time since he'd left his village, he hadn't had to choose between where he came from and where he was going.

He'd woven them together.

One beam at a time.

It was late when Vihaan stepped out of the annex. The corridors had gone quiet, emptied of students and sunlight. Only the hum of sodium lamps and the low buzz of insects kept the evening alive.

He found a quiet bench behind the mess hall, sat down, and dialed home.

Two rings.

Then Amma's voice, gentle and alert.

"Vihaan?"

"Hmm. Just wanted to say hi."

A pause.

"You ate?"

He smiled. "Yes. Mess food. You don't want the details."

She chuckled. "Then don't give me the recipe."

They talked for a few minutes idle things. The neighbor's new dog.

The grocery shop's roof leak. A sparrow nest above the kitchen light.

Then, almost as an afterthought, Vihaan said, "We're doing a project. Small-span bridge design. Coastal application."

"Oh," Amma said, interested. "Like the one near the estuary?"

He blinked. "You remember that?"

"Of course. You once scraped your knee there jumping from one beam to the other. Cried the whole walk home."

He laughed. "It was a big fall."

"You were five."

"Still counts."

A moment of soft silence.

Then she added, "You know, your Aachi used to draw hut plans in the sand. With a stick. After morning prayers, before she started cooking."

Vihaan's breath caught.

"She'd sit near the porch and trace rectangles and half-circles. One for the family. One for cows. A small one for drying clothes."

Vihaan closed his eyes.

"I didn't know that." "She said the beach was the only place she could build what she wanted. Even if the tide took it."

Vihaan stared into the darkness.

The tide.

Of course.

Not everything built was meant to last.

Some things were meant to begin.

"She never studied engineering," Amma said softly. "But she understood space better than anyone I've met."

"I think," Vihaan whispered, "she passed that down."

A longer pause now.

Then Amma said the one thing that would stay folded in Vihaan's chest forever:

"Kanna," Amma said, voice softer than a tide pulling back, "build the kind of bridge your Aachi would've crossed barefoot trusting the wood more than the water."

The line went quiet.

Not cut.

Just complete.

Vihaan sat there for a long time.

Not writing.

Not sketching.

Just holding.

Because sometimes, the strongest foundation isn't made of cement or steel.

It's made of a memory drawn in sand—

—held together by a woman who dreamed in blueprints no one ever taught her.

CHAPTER TEN

TO BUILD AND BE BUILT

The workshop smelled like effort sawdust, sweat, Fevicol all the ways dreams make themselves heavier before they stand. Vihaan stood just inside the threshold, taking it all in the echo of clinks and scrapes, the haze of chalk dust suspended in morning light, the rhythmic thunk-thunk of hammer meeting wood. Around the room, students crouched over half-finished models some whispering instructions, others arguing with rulers.

This was the messy middle.

Where ideas met gravity.

Their team had been assigned a workbench near the back, littered with leftover plywood scraps and a packet of rusting nails someone had forgotten to seal.

Aayush was already there sleeves rolled up, measuring tape flaring out like a tongue with something to prove.

Nikhil had a pencil tucked behind one ear and absolutely no plan. Meera arrived with the rolled schematic under one arm and two hair ties on her wrist one for her braid, one for whoever forgot theirs.

Vihaan placed his sketchbook down and looked at the materials before them.

MDF board.

Rebar sections.

Binding wire.

Not a bridge yet.

Not even bones.

Just potential, waiting to be wrangled.

"Alright," Aayush said briskly, "we follow the scaled base plan to a T. I'll start marking the beam junctions."

"Wait," Meera said, frowning. "Shouldn't we adjust for the foundation slope? Otherwise the load will skew."

"That's in Phase 2. We stabilize after initial fix."

Vihaan watched them volley terms, instinctively turning his sketchbook to double-check their assumption.

He hesitated.

Then traced a finger along one line gently.

"Your beam's heartbeat is out of step," Vihaan said quietly, tracing the 5mm drift with his fingertip. "Your measurement skips 5 mm on the center axis. If we follow it, the whole deck will skew by the second bay."

Silence.

Aayush paused. Re-checked.

He exhaled. "Right."

"Good catch," Meera murmured, almost like it was to herself.

Vihaan didn't beam. He just nodded and stepped back.

The first cut was made. The wood smelled sharp and clean. And suddenly, it was real.

A structure that had lived only in their heads now demanded hands. Mistakes would leave marks. Ideas would need glue. And time would not slow down for anyone.

Vihaan picked up a piece of sandpaper and began smoothing the beam edge. The rhythm calmed him.

Because in this noise, in this dust, in this imperfection he saw something that books never said:

To build something is to be unsure at first.

But still begin.

Aayush had been measuring the same cross beam for the third time in fifteen minutes.

"It's still two millimeters off," he muttered, frowning down at the ruler like it had betrayed him.

"It's within tolerance," Meera offered gently. "It won't affect load distribution on a scaled model."

"No. Precision is principle," Aayush said, not looking up. "If we let two millimeters go now, we'll let five go later."

Vihaan didn't reply.

Not yet.

He continued shaping the next support piece sanding gently, evening the edge where the grain had splintered.

Nikhil, nearby, whispered, "Bro's acting like we're sending this thing to ISRO."

Vihaan smiled, but his eyes stayed on the work.

Another ten minutes passed.

Aayush hovered over Meera's layout, corrected Nikhil's angle cut, rechecked the epoxy Vihaan was mixing.

The air was starting to feel thick not with heat, but tension.

Then came the tipping point.

Aayush moved one of Vihaan's aligned beam pairs by a sliver.

"I just want it straighter."

Vihaan paused.

Wiped his hands.

Then looked at Aayush not confrontational, but steady.

"Hold too tight," Vihaan said, voice steady, "and even the strongest structure forgets how to carry its own weight."

Aayush blinked.

"What?"

Vihaan repeated, slower. "Structures and people. Both need room to adjust. Breathe. We're building to show function, not control."

The workshop fell briefly still.

It wasn't the volume of Vihaan's voice. It was the evenness.

Like he wasn't trying to win an argument.

He was just telling the truth.

Meera looked at him for a second longer than usual.

Nikhil muttered, "Mic drop."

Aayush opened his mouth then closed it.

He stepped back.

"Okay," he said finally. "You align this joint."

Vihaan nodded.

No gloating.

No performance.

Just quiet leadership.

He didn't want to be right.

He wanted the bridge to hold.

And he was learning that sometimes, the strongest reinforcement isn't steel it's stillness.

The blueprint had smudged.

Not entirely. Just enough to warp one measurement a water droplet from someone's elbow, maybe, or the edge of a sweaty palm.

But in model-making, small mistakes have big echoes.

"Who redrew the support detail?" Meera snapped, voice taut as a string pulled too tight.

Everyone froze.

Nikhil looked up from the base grid. Aayush's hand stilled mid-mark. Vihaan, holding a wood strip between clamps, blinked once.

"I did," he said calmly.

Meera exhaled, sharp. "It's reversed. We'll have to redo that whole side."

Vihaan didn't flinch.

"Okay," he said. "We'll fix it."

"It's not just about fixing it," Meera said, rubbing her temple. "It's time, Vihaan. We're already behind on reinforcement joints, and the epoxy's drying too slow and—"

She stopped.

Her voice had cracked.

Not loud.

Just enough.

Vihaan looked at her not with apology, not with critique.

Just quiet recognition.

"Do you want to hear a dumb story?" he asked.

Meera blinked, caught off guard. "What?"

"About a goat. And a pile of bricks."

A pause.

Nikhil grinned. "Always."

Vihaan leaned against the bench.

"So when I was six, Aachi was building a new chicken coop. She stacked bricks neatly in a pile near the porch. Every day, I'd come home from school, and one brick would be out of place."

"Ghost?" Aayush offered dryly.

"Goat," Vihaan said. "A very stubborn goat who lived in the next house. She used to sneak over and rearrange the stack. One brick. Every single day."

Even Meera cracked a smile.

"One day, I got mad. Kicked the pile over. Told Aachi I was quitting chicken coop construction forever. She just laughed and said, "If you want to build anything real, kanna," Aachi had laughed, "you have to leave space for stubborn goats and sudden rains.""

The team chuckled.

The tension melted not in a rush, but like sugar in tea.

Vihaan picked up the smudged plan and laid it flat.

"I reversed one beam. We'll redo it. It's just a goat."

Meera exhaled again slower this time. The sharpness had left her posture.

"Sorry," she murmured. "I didn't mean to snap."

Vihaan shrugged gently. "Bridges don't fall from one loose nail. Neither do teams."

They got back to work.

And somewhere between clamps and cuts, Meera passed him a replacement strip their fingers brushed briefly.

No words.

But it was her way of saying: thank you.

The lab was nearly empty.

A single tube light buzzed overhead, flickering faintly more ghost than glow. Outside the windows, campus lights blinked like thoughts too tired to stay lit. The clink of metal echoed louder when no one else was around.

Vihaan stood over the half-built model, hands covered in chalk dust and resin.

Everyone else had left.

Aayush had needed dinner.

Nikhil had trailed after him, muttering something about Maggi and philosophy.

Meera had paused at the door.

"You staying?"

Vihaan had nodded.

She didn't press. Just said, "Don't forget to lock the resin."

Now, hours later, he knelt beside the structure.

One of the lateral braces wasn't aligning. A 5-degree tilt that would throw the whole deck into a subtle but certain imbalance.

He could've blamed the base cut.

Could've asked for help tomorrow.

Instead, he stayed.

Unscrewed. Re-cut. Replaced.

The sound of filing filled the room gritty and soft. Like waves reshaping a stone.

Vihaan didn't rush.

He worked with the slow attention of someone folding a letter they never planned to send just wanting it to be done right.

He remembered Aachi's fingers, trimming flower stems at dusk.

Do it once. Do it well.

The beam finally slid into place.

Flush. Clean. Holding.

Vihaan stepped back.

Not to admire.

Just... to see.

And what he saw wasn't perfect. It wasn't finished.

But it was his.

Not just because he'd helped design it.

Because he'd stayed.

When it was inconvenient.

When no one was watching.

When it would've been easier to leave it slightly crooked and hope no one noticed.

He wiped his palms on his jeans, leaving behind pale handprints.

Then reached for his notebook and wrote, in the margin beside a half-sketched truss:

The structure isn't strong because I know everything.

It's strong because I didn't walk away.

No one would ever read that line.

And somehow, that made it mean more.

By Thursday, the base was done.

Mostly.

The beams were in place, the joints cured overnight, the centerline finally respected.

But one connection the cross-bracing joint on the fourth pier kept slipping.

"It's like trying to tie a shoelace with one hand," Nikhil muttered, squinting at the misbehaving connection.

"Or trying to keep your towel from falling off while running for the bathroom light," Vihaan added without looking up.

Everyone paused.

Aayush snorted.

Then Nikhil burst out laughing. "Only you could civil-engineer that analogy."

Even Meera smiled.

The ice had long cracked. Now it was melting.

They gathered around the model.

The issue was clear the angle iron was slightly warped, probably during cutting. It needed either replacement (time they didn't have) or compensation through adjustment.

"What if we introduce a twin offset?" Vihaan suggested. "Use a secondary strip at the junction. Distribute the flex across two load points."

Aayush frowned. "Might work, but we'd need a flexible anchor."

"I can drill that," Meera said. "I have the high-speed bit."

They moved quickly.

Nikhil held the frame steady.

Meera drilled.

Vihaan cut and sanded the anchor plate. Aayush adjusted the tension wire on the brace.

Then gently, together they eased the support into place.

It fit.

Not just physically.

Perfectly.

The model didn't creak. It breathed.

As if it had been waiting to exhale.

Everyone stepped back.

For a beat, no one spoke.

Then Nikhil raised an invisible trophy. "We... are structural gods."

"Don't tempt fate," Aayush said, but he was smiling.

Vihaan leaned on the edge of the table, looking at the joined beam where four minds and six hands had brought something into alignment.

Not perfectly.

But harmoniously.

"Feels good, doesn't it?" Meera asked, brushing sawdust off her sleeve.

Vihaan nodded.

"Like we all left fingerprints in the same place."

She looked at him for a moment. "Exactly that."

And for the first time since this project began, Vihaan didn't feel like he had to earn his place in the group.

He just had to show up.

And show care.

By Friday evening, the model stood.

Not perfect.

But standing.

The skeletal structure had form now six piers, four trusses, an uneven but sincere deck. The base alignment was still a little off-center, one of the joints wore more glue than grace, and the paint was uneven in places. But it held together like something meant well not as an object, but as an intention.

"Okay," Nikhil said, standing back, hands on hips. "If this bridge were a person, it would be that cousin who's awkward at weddings but still makes everyone dance."

Meera chuckled. Even Aayush cracked a rare half-smile.

They stood around it quietly, like people visiting something sacred they'd accidentally created.

Vihaan didn't say much.

He didn't need to.

Because he recognized it.

This model crude edges and all still carried the memory of his first sketch. The curve of the beam, the asymmetry of the joints, the slightly bowed deck. Not copied. Not exact.

But inspired.

Meera turned to him. "It's yours, you know."

He shook his head. "It's all of ours."

Aayush looked at the base again. "Technically, it's only structurally sound because we—"

"Bro," Nikhil interrupted. "It's a metaphor. Let the moment breathe."

They laughed again and this time, it wasn't from relief or exhaustion. It was real.

They didn't win any recognition when the review came.

The panel liked the idea.

Critiqued the finish.

Said it "lacked polish."

And maybe they were right.

Some teams brought near-flawless models with laser-cut precision, miniature street lamps, and mirror-sheen paint jobs.

But none of that mattered much.

Because when Vihaan packed up the model after the presentation placed it in the cardboard box that still smelled faintly of sawdust and fevicol he realized what they'd really built:

A kind of home.

A structure made not of glue and balsa wood...

...but of conflict, compromise, shared laughter, and that first hesitant moment someone let you draw the lines.

On their way out of the hall, Meera walked beside him.

She didn't speak for a while.

Then, softly: "It wasn't the best model."

"No," Vihaan agreed. "But it held."

She looked at him.

"I think we all did."

He nodded.

And in that nod was something unspoken, something final the closing of a chapter, not in a notebook, but in the becoming of who they were.

CHAPTER ELEVEN

THE THINGS WE CAN'T CARRY

I t was a Sunday afternoon, the kind where the hostel felt split between post-lunch naps and overdue assignments. Vihaan had just returned from the library notebook under his arm, shirt sticking to his back from the heat when his phone buzzed.

Amma Calling.

He picked up with a quiet, "Hello?"

On the other end, joy unmistakable and unbothered by the distance.

"Guess what, kanna?" her voice beamed. "They started the Chariot Festival early this year!"

Vihaan paused. Blinked once.

"They did?"

"Mmm. The ratham came down the hill just now. Whole street is full of jasmine and sugarcane. I had to shout over the nadaswaram just to ask for vegetables!"

He could hear it in the background the low hum of drums, the far-off clang of a temple bell. Voices layered over laughter layered over home.

Amma kept describing it how the priest had tripped over his own veshti, how the twins from across the street had fought for the first coconut offering, how even the crows seemed louder today.

Vihaan listened. But something inside him had already started to pull away.

He was there.

But not there.

His memory didn't just recall it. It rebuilt it scent by scent, sway by sway until he could almost feel Aachi's hand tighten around his wrist again, her chant threading through the crowd like a lifeline. How she'd lift him slightly to see over people's heads. How her chant was the only one he ever trusted.

Now that same street was dancing without him.

The dust rising from the procession had forgotten his name.

"I'll send you photos," Amma said brightly. "They put up a new banner this year with lights! A bit flashy, but you know your father loves that sort of thing."

He smiled faintly.

"Okay," he said. "That'd be nice."

"You're quiet, kanna."

"Just... tired," he lied.

She paused not long. Just enough to know. Just enough to not press.

"Rest, then," she said softly. "And eat something warm tonight. You sound dry."

When the call ended, Vihaan sat still on the bed, phone resting face down beside him.

The room was too quiet. His chest too full.

He hadn't missed the festival.

The festival had missed him back. It was during a second call, the kind where Amma spoke more to the silence than to him.

Vihaan had been staring at his half-done assignment, his fingers idle on the keyboard, when her voice spilled through the speaker filling the gaps the way rasam fills a katori: gently, without asking.

"We finally got around to painting Aachi's corner, kanna."

His fingers paused mid-keystroke.

"What corner?"

"The prayer one," Amma said. "By the window. Where she used to light the lamp. The plaster was peeling."

Vihaan pictured it instantly not the plaster, but the light. That little strip of wall had always carried Aachi's thumbprint in sandalwood and ash. Her low chant every morning. The lamp's flame flickering even when the wind refused to stay outside.

"What color?" he asked, though he didn't know why.

"Pale yellow. Like morning."

He didn't reply.

Amma went on. "It looks nice now. Clean. Bright. We even bought a new brass diya."

Still, he said nothing.

Because in his memory, Aachi's lamp was clay.

Old.

Smudged.

Sacred in a way brass couldn't learn.

And that wall that small, cracked square of white limewash was not just paint. It was a story.

It held years.

It held her.

Now it is yellow, and Vihaan realized, sometimes grief isn't losing something.

It's realizing the world has already learned to live without it.

Vihaan nodded slowly, though Amma couldn't see.

"That's nice," he murmured.

"Hmm. I'll send you a photo," she said. "Don't worry. We didn't move the gods."

But Vihaan knew.

Something had shifted.

Later that evening, he sat alone in the library annex, book open but unread, mind floating somewhere between that yellow wall and the sound of matchsticks striking old wood.

He remembered how Aachi always painted around the gods, never over.

She believed some spaces remembered better when left untouched.

He understood now.

Because that wall had remembered her.

And in covering it, the house had not erased her, but translated her.

And Vihaan wasn't fluent in this new version.

Not yet.

The corridor echoed with laughter before Vihaan even reached the common room.

Inside, the ceiling fan whirred like a tired DJ while Nikhil danced or attempted to to an old Tamil remix blasting from someone's cracked Bluetooth speaker. Mukund tossed a balled-up sock at him mid-spin. Two first-years played carrom in the corner, while someone balanced a tin of Thums Up on a stack of textbooks.

Vihaan stepped in slowly.

The room pulsed with noise, joy, inside jokes that moved too fast to catch.

It was the kind of scene that usually made him smile or at least observe with quiet amusement.

But today, it felt like watching from underwater.

He stood by the doorway, one hand curled around the strap of his bag, unsure whether to step forward or back.

His chest still held the yellow of that newly painted wall.

It clashed with the room's neon.

Nikhil spotted him. "Aye, structural poet! Come we need a judge for 'worst dance move that could injure your ego and knees.'"

Vihaan tried to smile. "I'll disqualify everyone on ethical grounds."

Mukund cheered. "He speaks! The civil one emerges!"

They made space for him on the floor, but he didn't sit.

Just hovered.

The jokes flew over him like paper planes some made it halfway across, most didn't land.

Someone passed him a half-open packet of murukku.

He took it politely.

Didn't eat.

It wasn't sadness.

Just disconnection.

As if the frequency had shifted, and he could no longer tune in.

He stood near the window, watching lights flicker in another hostel block. Heard a train whistle far off, low and fading. Smelled the cheap deodorant someone had sprayed too generously.

And yet, he felt thousands of kilometers from here.

Not because anyone had pushed him away.

But because memory had gently pulled him back.

And then just when he thought he might slip out quietly Nikhil walked over, handed him a pillow, and said simply:

"Stay. You don't have to laugh. Just... sit."

Vihaan sat.

No one stared.

No one asked.

And in that quiet permission, something settled.

The ache didn't disappear.

But it had room now.

And Vihaan began to realize maybe loneliness wasn't always the absence of people.

Sometimes it was just grief that hadn't found its name yet.

The bus rattled forward part sigh, part lurch carrying tired students, open bags, loose earbuds, and the usual end-of-day fog.

Vihaan sat by the window, one leg tucked beneath the other, elbow resting on the sill. The breeze hit his cheek in stutters, warm and dry.

Outside, the road unfurled in a blur of electric poles, tea stalls, and marigold garlands drooping from wires.

But he wasn't seeing any of it.

His eyes were open.

But his mind was somewhere between the yellow paint in Aachi's corner and the taste of festival sugarcane he hadn't touched in two years.

In his lap, his notebook sat closed.

On the cover, a light smudge maybe from rasam. Maybe from glue. He didn't notice when the bus slowed. Didn't flinch when it paused.

Only when it groaned back into motion and the name of his stop vanished in the rearview mirror did Vihaan blink and sit up.

He'd missed it.

No panic.

No curse under breath.

Just quiet recognition.

I wasn't ready to return yet.

He got off at the next stop two bends down, near a mechanic shop and a paan stall that smelled like cloves and rubber.

The sun was dipping behind the tallest building on the block. Shadows stretched long and thin across the pavement like threads pulled too far.

Vihaan walked.

One hand in his pocket.

One thought following another.

He passed a group of schoolboys kicking a bottle like a football. A woman stringing roses into a garland on her doorstep. A tea vendor dusting off glass tumblers with the bottom of his shirt.

Life, as usual, moved without pause.

And yet, every sound felt dipped in softness. The kind that comes after loss not sharp anymore. Just suspended.

He passed a narrow side street and saw a wall covered in peeling movie posters. One had half a face, eyes smiling, mouth missing.

He stopped.

Took a photo of it without thinking.

Then kept walking.

By the time he reached the hostel gate, the sky had darkened into something that wasn't quite night that in-between hue where shadows and memory begin to look alike.

Vihaan didn't feel lost.

He didn't feel found either.

But he felt something shift inside him the way a column does when it learns to bear weight without complaint.

He whispered not to anyone, not for anyone just to the dusk:

"I didn't get off late. I just wasn't done arriving."

The stairwell always smelled faintly of wet socks, old dust, and something he couldn't name.

It was the most ordinary place in the hostel chipped tiles, fluorescent light that flickered like it was remembering how to glow, and a crack down the side of the wall that had grown since monsoon.

Vihaan sat on the fourth step from the bottom.

Not for any reason.

It just felt like the step that understood.

He hadn't turned on his phone. Didn't open his notebook.

Just sat. Palms resting on his knees. Shoulders loose with the weight of memory, not yet sadness just the early ache of remembering something long enough that it starts to sting.

He didn't hear the footsteps until they were close.

Then a voice soft, familiar.

"I brought you murukku," Meera said.

He looked up.

She stood holding a crumpled paper pouch. No smile. No questions.

She sat beside him one step higher, knees close.

Neither of them spoke for a minute.

Then Vihaan took a breath, the kind that starts somewhere near the ribs.

"When I was nine," he said, "Aachi and I had this fight."

Meera didn't respond. Just turned slightly toward him.

"She wanted to teach me the Vishnu Sahasranamam. I didn't want to learn it. Said it was too long. Too slow. That my friends were playing cricket and I didn't want to chant slokas like an old man."

He smiled faintly. "I shouted at her. Said her god wasn't mine."

Meera's face softened, but still no words.

"She didn't speak to me for a day," Vihaan continued. "I thought she was angry."

He looked down at his fingers, flexing lightly in his lap.

"But that night, after I fell asleep, she tucked a piece of coconut burfi under my pillow."

A long pause.

"I found it in the morning. With a note on rice paper."

"What did it say?" Meera asked, finally.

Vihaan swallowed.

"It said, 'Even if you don't chant the gods, kanna, I still do. For you.'" Meera looked straight ahead.

And whispered, "That's the kind of love that makes you who you are before you even realize it."

He nodded.

A soft gust of air swept through the stairwell carrying with it the faint scent of her jasmine oil and something sweet from the mess downstairs.

Vihaan didn't cry.

But something in his chest loosened.

And in that pause between silence and speech, he realized:

He hadn't shared that memory with anyone before.

And now it lived in someone else, too.

The knock came just before dinner.

Three soft taps on the door hesitant, like the person behind it wasn't sure whether to wait or walk away.

Vihaan opened it to find Mukund standing there, awkward as always, holding a small steel dabba with rubber bands around it.

"From the warden's office," he said. "Someone left it for you. Said it came through a family friend on campus."

Vihaan stared at the dabba.

It was dented on one side, with a white cloth tied tightly around the lid. He knew that cloth. It had been part of an old kitchen towel at home Aachi used to tear squares from it to hold hot vessels.

He untied it slowly, like unwrapping memory.

Inside: rasam.

Not restaurant rasam. Not hostel mess rasam.

But home rasam.

The color was deeper. The curry leaves curled slightly at the edge. The tamarind not too sharp. And it smelled like firewood and afternoons and the sound of ladles scraping the bottom of old vessels.

There was a note tucked between the lid and the rim stained slightly with turmeric at the corners.

> "*Kanna,*
> *You sounded tired on the phone.*
> *So I asked Uma aunty to send this through her cousin's son. He works near your college.*
> *Don't forget to heat it. Add rice. Eat slowly.*
> *Some warmth doesn't travel well but this one might.*
> *– Amma*"

Vihaan sat on the floor, back against the wall, katori cradled in both hands.

He didn't speak.

Didn't need to.

Each sip stitched something broken inside him not hunger, not loneliness, but the small, aching spaces where memory made its nest.

It didn't fix anything.

Didn't bring Aachi back.

Didn't repaint the corner white.

Didn't rewind time to a festival he could dance in again.

But it acknowledged it.

His ache. His distance. His trying.

And sometimes, that's all grief asks for.

After dinner, he returned to his desk, opened his sketchbook, and flipped past diagrams and measurements and pages filled with bridge joints and column loads until he reached a blank page.

And then, slowly, he began to draw.

Not from imagination.

But from remembrance.

A corner.

Whitewashed. Slightly cracked.

A clay lamp, not brass. The kind Aachi touched with reverence, never polish.

A string of jasmine hung unevenly. A wall that held the scent of camphor and turmeric.

He shaded gently, softly. Every line a blessing, every stroke a prayer in pencil.

At the bottom, he didn't sign his name.

He simply wrote:

Some walls crumble.

Some lamps burn out.

But the spaces they blessed still flicker inside us alive, golden, and waiting.

He closed the book, not with finality, but with care.

And as he turned off the light, a breeze crept in through the half-open window.

Soft. Familiar.

Like something from far away had made its way back.

And settled.

Right beside him.

CHAPTER TWELVE

THE PEOPLE WHO STAY

Mornings had begun to change. Not in the weather Mumbai's heat still wrapped itself around the hostel like a thick, stubborn shawl no one dared to wash but in the way Vihaan moved through them.

He woke earlier now.

Before the first slippers scraped across the corridor.

Before alarms began their symphony of half-snores and curses.

Before the sun decided whether it even wanted to rise today.

And in that blue-grey hush when the world belonged only to those too humble to claim it Vihaan learned something new about living:

Healing doesn't always announce itself.

Sometimes it sweeps quietly across wet tiles.

From the landing, he leaned against the rusted railing and watched.

The old cleaning woman sari tucked up one side, bangles clinking softly drew her broom in rhythmic arcs across the courtyard. Each stroke seemed less about dust and more about memory.

She paused near the neem tree, stooped down, and with delicate fingers fingers that looked carved from monsoon and work tucked a fallen flower behind her ear.

It wasn't showy.

It wasn't sentimental.

It was a queen's coronation that only the morning sky was privileged to witness.

Vihaan smiled without knowing he was smiling.

Down below, the mess boy wrestled once more with the eternally leaking tap wrench twisting, curse muttered, water spitting defiantly. The leak had been there longer than some first-years.

And still, every day, Ravi returned unrolling plumber's tape that stuck to itself, humming songs too old for the radio, tightening bolts as if they were tiny promises he refused to break.

These weren't the professors.

Not the mentors.

Not the friends who texted at midnight before exams.

But somehow they were his people.

The ones who stayed.

Who showed up without applause, without certificates, without even being asked.

He thought of Aachi.

How she had swept the veranda every evening not as a chore, but as prayer, disguised in movement.

Maybe, Vihaan thought, belonging isn't a chorus of voices calling your name.

Maybe it's the way someone saves a seat for you without asking.

He reached for his sketchbook.

Not to capture the cracked plaster or the sagging roof.

Not to draw the courtyard itself.

No.

Today, he drew her hands wide palms, steady fingers cradling the broom like an old companion.

He drew the leaking tap mid-drip catching a sliver of stubborn sunlight.

He drew the small flower tucked into her hair, leaning like a lullaby against her temple.

His pencil moved slowly.

No rush.

No ache.

Just... gratitude, sketching itself into being.

Later that morning, the tap sputtered in protest again.

Vihaan usually walked past it without a thought.

Today, he stopped.

"You want a hand?" he asked, crouching beside Ravi.

The boy looked up, eyebrows raised, then grinned.

"You know plumbing, boss?"

"No," Vihaan admitted. "But I can hold things."

Ravi tossed him the spanner.

"Hold it like your mother's bangles not too tight. They'll slip."

Vihaan laughed. And he obeyed.

They worked in companionable silence tightening, adjusting, coaxing stubborn metal to yield. The tiles beneath them were damp and smelled of rust and old patience.

When the leak slowed to a lazy drip, they sat back.

"What's your name?" Vihaan asked.

"Ravi," the boy said. "You?"

"Vihaan."

A pause.

A smile.

"I saw that sketch once," Ravi said, wiping his hands. "The old lady with the lamp. On the temple wall near the annex."

Vihaan blinked.

"She looked," Ravi added, "like someone who kept stories warm for when the right person came looking."

Vihaan's throat tightened, gently.

"She did," he said quietly. "She was my grandmother."

Ravi nodded the kind of nod that doesn't pretend to know sorrow but respects it anyway.

"You ever need an extra hand," Ravi grinned, standing up, "call me."

"Same to you," Vihaan replied.

Sometimes, friendship isn't forged over years.

Sometimes, it's passed silently, like a wrench between hands.

At exactly 7:02 AM, the mess bell rang.

Not at seven.

Not at five past.

Always — always — at 7:02.

The clang echoed across the courtyard, startling pigeons and dragging sleepy bodies out of doorways. It was as dependable as sunrise. As irritating as exams.

Vihaan had never cared who rang it.

Until one bleary morning, half-clutching a mug of unfinished coffee, he saw him.

A boy.

Maybe a first-year.

Hair clipped too short. Watch slipping loose around his wrist.

He walked up to the brass bell outside the mess, checked his oversized blue watch, waited two solemn breaths, and rang it with the dignity of a priest calling morning prayers.

Then walked away without ceremony.

Vihaan watched the ritual unfold again the next day.

And the next.

One morning, the boy arrived early. Stood there, hands clasped behind his back, waiting as if bearing witness to the exact second the world spun forward.

And at the moment ordained by some unseen temple clock inside his heart:

Clang.

And he was gone.

It wasn't about punctuality.

It was about giving the day permission to begin.

Later, in the safety of his room, Vihaan drew him a slender silhouette beside a giant bell carved from open sky, his watch face not numbered but filled with waves and clouds and rice grains.

Below it, Vihaan wrote:

Not all anchors are heavy.

Some wear blue straps and ring mornings into being.

That Sunday, Vihaan didn't leave his room.

Not out of sadness.

Not out of loneliness.

Just to be still.

He pulled the curtain aside, letting sunlight pool across the floor in crooked golden ladders. The air smelled of soap, wet concrete, someone else's paratha frying somewhere out of reach.

And Vihaan wrote.

Not for class.

Not for Aachi.

Not for anyone who would ever grade or remember it.

Just for himself.

Healing is not a sudden light.

It is the mess boy's wrench tightening against the leak.

It is the cleaning woman's flower tucked into battle-worn hair.

It is the boy with a too-big watch ringing mornings into being.

None of them shouted their names into my life.

They just stayed long enough to be written into me.

He sat back.

Exhaled.

In that moment, Vihaan understood what Aachi had once whispered while packing pickle into a jar:

"We don't always choose our prayers, kanna.

Sometimes, we live them."

That evening, Vihaan wandered back to the courtyard.

The old woman swept a stray leaf from the path and nodded without looking up.

Ravi tightened the stubborn pipe with one hand and waved with the other.

The bell boy struck 7:02 with military devotion, sending another day forward.

Vihaan didn't need to say anything.

But inside him, a soft thank you echoed slow and sure threading itself into the spaces that used to ache.

He smiled.

Not because everything had healed.
But because something had quietly begun.
And sometimes, that's all the morning asks of you:
To notice who stayed, even when you forgot to.

CHAPTER THIRTEEN

MEERA'S MAP

The wheels hummed like a lullaby gone slightly off-key a song stitched from potholes and half-forgotten conversations. The college bus dragged itself out of the city like a reluctant creature, pausing at every dent and divot in the road, as if reconsidering the journey altogether.

It was only 6:30 in the morning, and the sky still wore its softest blue the color of hesitation, of days not yet decided.

Vihaan sat by the window.

As he always did.

Not for the view.

But for the permission to turn away from the world without apology a quiet alcove to think, to drift, without explaining the shape of his silence.

Beside him, Meera.

She hadn't said a word since boarding.

Her braid was slightly unraveled at the end, strands escaping like they, too, refused to be bound this early. Her fingers rested lightly on a closed notebook in her lap, unmoving, as though even they had agreed to honor the stillness.

They hadn't chosen to sit together.

They just had.

The way rivers sometimes run parallel without needing a map to tell them how.

The wind from the open window brushed against them teasing a sleeve here, grazing a forehead there. The bus rocked gently, the tired engine humming, the world slipping past in muted colors.

Neither of them spoke.

And yet, the silence was a conversation all its own full, breathing, waiting.

Vihaan opened his sketchbook without thinking.

The page turned to a fresh, blank sheet a space unclaimed, like the morning.

He didn't draw her.

That would have been too much. Too loud for a moment stitched in whisper.

Instead, his pencil moved to capture the road ahead the bend, the downward slope, the way the earth seemed to fall away just before a grove of trees swallowed the horizon.

A road that didn't know exactly where it was going.

And trusted the curve anyway.

That's when Meera spoke.

"Some roads," she murmured, voice low and unhurried, "look like they're trying to escape something."

Vihaan's pencil paused midair.

"And some," he said, "look like they're chasing what they already lost."

She turned, just slightly enough for him to catch the faintest curve of a smile ghosting her lips.

The bus hit a bump.

Her hand brushed against his forearm.

Neither moved away.

Ahead, the ocean unfurled suddenly between two crooked coconut palms startlingly blue, impossibly wide. A glimpse of forever, caught between the casual edges of earth.

Meera leaned toward the window, her gaze softening.

"When I was little," she said, "I thought the ocean only existed when I could see it. Like it was waiting for me."

Vihaan's eyes found the horizon.

"Maybe it still is," he whispered.

And then the silence returned.

Not empty but full of all the words that didn't need saying.

The bus rolled on.

And something unwritten unfolded between them a map without labels, a journey without destinations.

The fort rose like a crumbling prayer at the edge of the world stubborn, salt-bitten, etched with the sighs of centuries.

Its walls wore moss and graffiti with equal indifference.

Its stones remembered footsteps long forgotten by the feet that made them.

The group scattered quickly professors pointing at arches, classmates chasing selfies, voices bouncing off cannon-marked walls.

Vihaan and Meera, walking slower than the rest, turned a corner too late.

The others vanished swallowed by doorless rooms and sun-dappled shadows.

"I think we're lost," Vihaan said, though without any urgency.

Meera surveyed the quiet.

"Maybe we're just the ones who stayed long enough to see what was worth getting lost for."

They didn't call out.

They didn't retrace their steps.

They simply walked toward wherever the silence would allow.

The corridor narrowed and then unfurled into a clearing a courtyard open to the sky, stitched with wild grass and crowned by a broken stepwell at its center.

No one else.

Just the hush of wind, the murmur of distant waves, and the steady thrum of something softer than discovery.

Meera sat on the rim of the dry well, tracing its rough edge with her fingers.

"I used to be terrified of being forgotten," she said, almost absently.

"Like if I stopped proving I mattered, even for a minute, the world would just... move on."

Vihaan sat beside her close enough to share breath, but far enough to leave space.

She didn't wait for a response.

"I kept a chart once," she continued. "Twelve years old. Every achievement, every medal, every rank. Like a maintenance log... for my worth."

Vihaan bent down, picked up a fallen leaf dry, veined like an old palm.

"Maps are good," he said softly. "Until they stop showing you the way home."

She looked at him then really looked and something between them shifted, not forward, not backward, but deeper.

"I thought you were the quiet one," she said.

"I am," Vihaan smiled. "But even quiet people draw maps to find themselves again."

She smiled back not performative, not polished.

Just real.

And for the first time, the fort didn't feel abandoned.

It felt inhabited not by history, but by two souls, finding a place to belong.

The fort's crumbling edge sloped toward a hidden crescent beach no umbrellas, no souvenir stalls, no footprints.

Just salt.

Wind.

And the slow breathing of the earth meeting the sea.

Vihaan and Meera slipped off their shoes, letting sand gather between their toes like forgotten blessings.

No professors.

No classmates.

Just the two of them, and a sky too vast to name.

Vihaan knelt by a patch of dry sand, drawing quick lines with a stick spirals, arrows, loops that ended in nowhere.

Meera crouched beside him.

"What is it?" she asked.

"A map," he said.

"To where?"

He looked up, smiling.

"To you."

She laughed a laugh without walls and watched as he traced her, not in lines or likeness, but in memories imagined and feelings unnamed.

"This spiral," he said, pointing, "is where you plan things three steps ahead."

"This X," he said, tapping, "is where you hide your exhaustion under sarcasm."

"And this," he finished, swirling the center, "is where you forget to be cautious. And just glow."

Meera added a tiny heart near the swirl.

"You missed a part," she said.

"Maybe," Vihaan said. "Maybe some maps are better unfinished."

They watched as the tide, patient and inevitable, crept closer blurring the edges, forgiving the details, folding the drawing back into earth and water.

Because some moments are too sacred to frame.

They are meant only to be carried.

The sun dropped lower.

The tide whispered its way across the last of the sand sketch dissolving it not with violence, but with reverence.

Meera picked up a small lavender shell imperfect, weathered and placed it in Vihaan's hand.

A gift.

A memory.

A way of saying: I was here with you.

He closed his fingers around it gently.

Neither said the obvious goodbyes.

Because the sea had taught them:

Some things don't end.

They just slip into the next wave.

The bus ride back was quieter — not heavy, not hollow.

Just... full.

The kind of full that doesn't clamor for conversation.

Meera rested her head lightly against the window, breath fogging the glass in slow, steady intervals.

Vihaan sat beside her, notebook closed, shell tucked safely in his pocket.

When he returned to his room, the world outside had faded to velvet stitched with the faintest stars.

He opened his sketchbook.

The page from the morning the road bending into uncertainty waited for him.

But now, in the corner, in neat, looping handwriting that wasn't his own, he found a line:

"You see things others forget to name."

— M.

Vihaan smiled not a wide smile.

A small, quiet one.

The kind that says: I found something today I didn't know I was looking for.

He closed the book gently.

Placed the shell beside it.

A keepsake.

Not just of a day,

or a fort,

or a beach.

But of something far rarer:

The feeling of being seen and the quiet promise to never lose the way back.

TO FAIL AND BE FORGIVEN

The sun was already high when Vihaan finally looked at the calendar tacked to his wall.

It wasn't the date that caught him. It was the circled word in red ink.

Submission: Soils Lab – Final Draft.

His pen had written it. Neat. Clear.

But somehow, his memory hadn't followed.

He stood frozen, the toothbrush still in his hand, foam drying at the corners of his mouth. It was already 9:10 AM.

The deadline was 9:00.

For a full minute, Vihaan didn't move.

His body flushed not with heat, but with that strange, slow wave that begins in the chest and rises to the ears. The kind that makes everything sound farther away. A buzz without bees.

No.

He opened his laptop. Clicked. Refreshed. Checked the portal.

Closed.

He hadn't submitted.

The document sat neatly in his drafts folder. Fully written. Proofread. Even paginated. A report he'd spent nights perfecting forgotten, not because of laziness, not because of arrogance...

...but because his mind had been elsewhere.

On drawings. On Meera's sketchbook note. On the memory of Aachi's voice murmuring in his sleep.

He closed the laptop, gently.

Sat on his bed.

And stared at nothing.

For someone else, this might have been a minor inconvenience. A chance to request an extension. But for Vihaan, it felt existential.

Not because of the grade.

But because he had never — not once — let something slip like this before.

He remembered the way his father once scolded him for a missed bus in class 9. How he'd stood silently as his mother folded the tiffin she'd made with too much care. How Aachi had whispered that evening, "Even temples close late sometimes. You are allowed."

But this didn't feel like that.

This felt like the unraveling of a thread he wasn't supposed to tug.

Vihaan leaned back on the bed.

The fan spun overhead, indifferent.

Outside, someone shouted over a cricket ball that had gone too far.

The hostel life continued, unaware.

But inside him a voice.

One he hadn't heard in a while.

You're slipping.

You're not built for this.

What would she think of you now?

He didn't argue.

Didn't move.

He just stared at the spot on the wall where sunlight hit and realized...

...it looked an awful lot like guilt.

Vihaan didn't go to class that day.

He told himself he needed time to think. To draft an apology. To figure out the right words that didn't sound like an excuse. But mostly, he needed to disappear.

He skipped lunch too wandered aimlessly around campus, careful to walk the long way around the civil block, where Professor Bhargava's office sat with its half-drawn blinds and a fading sticker that read "Build with Intent."

Even the slogan felt like a quiet accusation now.

He spent two hours in the library, not reading.

The book in front of him was open to a page on soil bearing capacity, but the words had lost their shape. Letters blurred. Paragraphs floated. He found himself tracing the edge of a diagram without really knowing why.

Around him, people moved with purpose printing notes, whispering answers, chasing deadlines. The kind of energy that used to comfort him.

Today, it only deepened the ache.

He couldn't shake the feeling that he'd cracked something inside himself.

Not big enough to break him.

But enough to feel the shift.

This isn't like you, the voice said.

You're slipping. You're forgetting who you were raised to be.

A boy who remembered deadlines.

Who double-checked time zones.

Who packed early, submitted early, studied late. A boy who never needed second chances. He thought of Aachi again; not her words, but her gaze. She had a way of looking at him that made him feel like he was more than what he achieved.

But today, he couldn't look himself in the mirror.

At one point, he walked past the department hallway and saw Professor Bhargava stepping out of his cabin, a file tucked under one arm.

Vihaan ducked instinctively behind a notice board.

He hated the gesture as soon as he did it.

But he stayed hidden.

Because shame is strange like that it makes you hide from the people who might forgive you first.

He stood there until the hallway was quiet again.

Then walked back to his room.

Slowly.

Like someone returning to a place he didn't feel worthy of.

The call came just as the light in Vihaan's room turned the color of cardamom that mellow, golden hue that made even silence seem scented.

He was lying on his bed, fully dressed but barefoot, eyes fixed on the ceiling fan as it spun like an unanswered question.

His phone vibrated once.

Then again.

A name flashed on the screen.

Prof. Bhargava.

His stomach dropped.

For a moment, he considered not answering. Letting it ring out. Pretending to be in class. Or asleep. Or invisible.

But he knew better.

He picked up. "Sir?"

A pause. Then the familiar, clipped voice not stern, not warm, just neutral.

"Vihaan. You didn't submit your soils report."

"I—I know, sir. I... forgot." The words felt too small for the weight they carried.

"I see."

Another pause.

Vihaan braced for a lecture. A deduction. A disappointment he'd carry like luggage.

But instead, Bhargava asked, "Are you free now?"

"Yes, sir."

"Come to my office."

Click.

The walk there felt longer than usual. The corridor stretched like time itself had slowed to make room for dread. He knocked gently.

"Come in," the professor called.

Bhargava sat at his desk, glasses pushed up, a red pen in hand. The fan above him creaked in a rhythmic lull.

Vihaan stepped in, spine straight, eyes lowered.

"I know this isn't like you," Bhargava said without looking up.

Vihaan opened his mouth, but Bhargava raised a hand.

"I'm not asking for an explanation."

Vihaan swallowed.

"I missed a submission once," Bhargava said, finally meeting his eyes. "Third semester. Strength of Materials. I'd lost a friend the week before. Didn't tell anyone. Just missed it."

Vihaan blinked.

"I thought it was the end of my credibility. My image. My rhythm." He leaned back.

"But sometimes, Vihaan, missing something doesn't mean you're losing everything. It just means..." He paused. "It just means you're human."

The word landed like a stone in a still lake.

Bhargava continued, voice gentler now. "Submit it late. I'll deduct the minimum. But only if you rewrite it not for me. For you."

Vihaan nodded slowly.

Bhargava looked down at his papers again.

"A good structure isn't perfect because it never cracks. It's good because we know how to repair it. That's the whole point of civil engineering, isn't it?"

Vihaan smiled, but it reached his eyes slowly.

"Thank you, sir."

Bhargava didn't reply. Just nodded toward the door.

As Vihaan stepped out, the hallway felt different.

Lighter.

As if forgiveness had opened a window.

The corridor outside Professor Bhargava's office smelled faintly of chalk and old paper.

Vihaan walked slowly, his hand brushing against the rail as if steadying himself not from shame but from something else.

Relief.

Not the loud kind. Not the shout-it-from-the-rooftop kind.

But the kind that feels like a held breath finally exhaled into stillness. Back in his room, he didn't open his laptop. Not yet.

He took out his notebook the one not for class, not for sketches the one Aachi had gifted before his first day with the inscription: For everything that doesn't fit into the syllabus.

He opened to a blank page.

At the top, he wrote:

""A good structure isn't perfect because it never cracks.

It's good because we know how to repair it." — Prof. Bhargava"

He stared at the sentence.

Wrote it again. Slower this time.

Underlined "repair."

Then sat back and closed his eyes.

For years, Vihaan had believed in rigidity. That strength meant not bending, not faltering, not forgetting. That to be dependable meant never dropping the thread never showing the soft underbelly of being human.

But now, something shifted.

What if... the blueprint wasn't supposed to be flawless?

What if the beauty of engineering of living was in knowing how to reinforce the weak spots? To fill the cracks with something stronger, not shame?

His fingers curled around the edge of the notebook.

He thought of bridges.

Of beams.

Of coastal homes that swayed with the wind, not against it.

Maybe that's what he was learning.

Not how to avoid failure.

But how to hold it gently.

And begin again.

The cursor blinked like breath.

Steady.

Unrushed.

Vihaan sat with his fingers poised, not anxious anymore, but... reverent. He hadn't opened the old draft. Hadn't copied from it. This wasn't about recreating what had already been.

This was about writing again knowing what he now knew.

So he began.

Not with precision.

But with intention.

Each sentence came slowly, but with a weight that felt earned. He didn't obsess over formatting. Didn't pause over typos. He let the knowledge flow the way it had always been inside him only now, unburdened by fear.

He diagrammed soil retention curves like memories he could now name.

Cited research like rituals.

Built conclusions like he would build walls stable, breathable, open to light.

It took him two hours.

But it didn't feel like a task.

It felt like... forgiveness in motion.

When he was done, he scrolled back to the top.

He didn't write his name.

Not yet.

Instead, he typed a single line, in small, italic font, just beneath the title:

> "*This version is not perfect.*
>   *But neither am I.*
>   *And maybe that's why it matters.*"

Then he saved it.

And closed the laptop.

Not with relief.

But with something gentler.

Something quieter.

A kind of peace.

he next morning, the sky was the colour of rice water soft, pale, undecided.

Vihaan dressed quietly.

Pressed his shirt.

Tied his shoelaces without overthinking the knots.

He didn't rehearse any explanations. Didn't carry an apology on his tongue. What he carried was a printed copy of the rewritten report, folded neatly into his file, and a resolve that wasn't loud just anchored.

As he stepped into the civil block, the familiar scent of cement dust and rusted stair rails wrapped around him like an old song. He passed the display wall of model bridges from previous years. They had always looked more like trophies than student projects glossy, perfect, untouched.

Today, they didn't intimidate him.

They reminded him that real structures live with stress.

And stand anyway.

He reached the classroom early.

Only a few students were scattered across the benches, heads bowed in soft rituals of morning review shuffling notes, adjusting pens, whispering last-minute answers to no one in particular.

Vihaan walked in.

Not like someone returning from exile.

Not like someone seeking validation.

Just... Vihaan.

He slid into his seat, took out his notebook, and placed it gently in front of him. One page fluttered open the one where Meera's note had been. The corners still carried the faintest curl.

He didn't close it.

Let it stay open beside his pen.

Like a quiet reminder:

You're allowed to show up without being flawless.

When Professor Bhargava entered, their eyes met briefly.
No nod.
No signal.
But Vihaan saw it the flicker of acknowledgment.
And for the first time in days, he smiled.
Not because everything was okay.
But because he was.
Exactly as he was.
And that... was enough.

CHAPTER FIFTEEN

HOUSES BUILT ON MEMORY

The letter came folded twice, its edges slightly frayed, its ink beginning to blur where a drop of water had once kissed it. It was tucked between a campus notice and a hostel electricity bill on the common board. A thin envelope. Addressed by hand.

Vihaan almost missed it.

His name was written in a familiar script careful, rounded Tamil letters. His mother's handwriting, unmistakably. And inside, another letter, this one older. Faded. From the headmaster of his old school in the village.

"Dear Vihaan,

It brings me quiet pride to invite you back to speak to our students.

Your story has become something they whisper about between classes a boy from our bench, now learning to build in Bombay.

Come. Tell them what is possible when silence is made of stone and sea."

There was no seal. No formality. Just a phone number and a date.

Next Saturday. Morning assembly.

Vihaan read it twice.

The first time, he felt a twinge of awkwardness he wasn't a celebrity, not even close. He hadn't won awards or published papers or led protests. Just a third-year engineering student, still figuring out how to hold himself together after late nights and small failures.

The second time he read it, his hands trembled.

Because something about it called.

Not just the words.

But the weight of being remembered by a place he thought he'd quietly left behind.

He folded the letter gently.

Placed it on his desk beside his sketchbook.

And for a long moment, he sat in silence, letting the idea take shape.

Not as a duty.

Not as an ego trip.

But as a kind of return.

To a classroom with uneven benches.

To the smell of chalk dust and rusted fans.

To the boy who once wrote dreams in the back of his math notebook and dared to fold them into paper planes.

He looked out the window.

The breeze was softer that evening.

Almost like permission.

The village hadn't changed much.

The same cracked road leading in like an afterthought.

The same tea stall with its lazy ceiling fan turning slower than thought.

Even the same stray dog limping along the temple wall, his ears half-torn but eyes sharp with memory.

Vihaan got off the bus with his duffel bag slung over one shoulder and a modest satchel of notes in the other. He hadn't told anyone back home he was coming. Not Amma. Not Appa. Not even the neighbors who would've surely arranged tea and biscuits and seventeen questions before he'd stepped off the porch.

He wanted this to be his first step.

His own.

The school stood at the far edge of the village still painted in that familiar pale yellow, faded to something closer to sunlight diluted in rainwater. The boundary wall leaned slightly inward, like it had tired of holding itself upright, but refused to fall.

A teacher met him near the staff room. "You've grown taller," she said, though she barely reached his shoulder. "But you still walk like you're afraid of waking the ground."

He bowed slightly in respect.

They led him to the assembly courtyard.

Nothing had changed.

The banyan tree still stood at the far corner, its roots curling into the earth like sleeping fingers. The prayer bell still hung crookedly, suspended from a nail that looked older than most of the students. The classrooms had no doors. Just curtains fluttering like breath.

And in that moment, Vihaan wasn't Ninteen.

He was eleven again in mismatched socks, dust on his knees, and a heart that beat faster every time a teacher said his name out loud.

He turned in a slow circle.

Let the air settle around him.

The school hadn't changed.

But he had.

And somehow, that made the moment feel sacred.

The courtyard was full now.

Rows of children seated cross-legged on the cracked cement, fidgeting with ribbons, scratching the backs of their knees, tugging at socks that wouldn't stay up. Some looked bored. Some curious. One or two stared up at the sky like they had better things to do than listen to someone from a world they hadn't touched yet.

Vihaan stood before them with no mic, no podium, no prepared speech.

Just dust on his shoes and a story folded somewhere between his ribs.

The headmaster introduced him briefly "a bright student from our school, now studying civil engineering in Mumbai, an example of what is possible" and then stepped back.

Vihaan looked at the faces in front of him.

Some reminded him of classmates long gone. Some looked exactly like the boy he used to be. And all of them, in some strange way, looked like hope waiting to be named.

He cleared his throat.

"I used to sit right where you are," he began, his voice calm but certain. "Not just in this school. On this very stone."

The children looked up.

He smiled. "Back then, I thought engineers were people who wore hard hats and built skyscrapers. I didn't know engineering could also be about holding a piece of your home in your hand and asking, 'How do I carry this into the world?'"

Someone sneezed. A few giggled. A small boy in the third row tried to copy his stance.

Vihaan continued, softer now.

"I once failed a math test and cried under that banyan tree. I thought that was the end of everything. But Aachi said, 'Crying is also a way of building, kanna. It's how you water the part of you that grows later.'"

The courtyard fell still.

Even the wind seemed to pause.

"I don't remember every grade I got here," Vihaan admitted. "But I remember how it felt when someone believed I could be more than I thought I was."

He stepped back, nodded toward the group.

"So if no one's told you lately let me be the first."

He pointed to the boy who had tried to mimic his stance. "You. With the crooked badge. You could design better roads than I ever will." The boy blinked, startled.

"To the girl in the last row the one who hasn't stopped doodling in her notebook? I hope you never stop drawing. It's not a distraction. It's a beginning."

He paused.

Then added, almost in a whisper:

"Whatever you dream build it. Even if no one claps. Even if it cracks. Build anyway."

There was no applause.

Just quiet.

The kind that meant they heard him.

And maybe, even more importantly... that they believed him.

After the talk, as the children dispersed some still looking back at him with wide eyes, others already chasing each other around the banyan tree — the headmaster called Vihaan into the staff room.

It smelled the same as it had a decade ago: of chalk dust, filter coffee, and sun-warmed wood. The shelves were lined with registers so thick they looked like they carried the weight of entire lifetimes.

"I thought you might like this," the headmaster said, reaching into a drawer and pulling out a thin manila folder. He slid it across the desk like something precious.

Vihaan opened it slowly.

Inside was a single page. Faint pencil. A heading scrawled in his unmistakable childhood hand.

Class Journal: What I Want to Build One Day.

— Vihaan S.

The moment he saw it, something tightened in his chest.

He hadn't remembered writing it. But the letters were his. The loops, the slightly crooked S's, the way he always forgot to leave space between words when excited.

He began to read.

""One day I want to build a house that feels like a hug.

It will have a porch for grandparents, and a kitchen that smells like Sundays.

There will be shelves for dreams, and secret corners where people can cry if they want to.

It won't be big. But it will never be empty.""

Vihaan felt the paper tremble in his hands.

The words blurred, not from time but from the sudden, unannounced tears that rose and fell without ceremony.

The headmaster said nothing. Just sipped his coffee and looked out the window, giving the moment space to breathe.

Vihaan folded the page gently. Tucked it into his satchel as though returning a piece of himself to its rightful place.

He didn't speak for a long time.

But inside him, something long dormant had just stirred.

A memory.

A mission.

A voice he hadn't heard in years.

And it said, simply:

Begin again.

The sun was beginning to lean west when Vihaan stood at the gate of his childhood home.

It looked smaller now.

Not in size, but in stature the way childhood places do when measured against grown-up shoulders and years passed.

The whitewash had faded into a tired cream. The coconut tree out front leaned slightly more. The bougainvillea, once trimmed with his father's old sickle, now spilled wild over the gate like it had given up being tamed.

He hadn't meant to come.

But his feet, familiar with these lanes in a way GPS could never be, had carried him here as if on instinct.

He pushed the gate gently. It creaked the same way it always had a long, slow sigh that seemed to recognize him.

The house was locked.

But the veranda was open.

He stepped onto it, each footfall stirring old dust, like turning pages of a story that still remembered its lines.

The swing where Aachi had sat every evening was gone. But the nails that once held it still clung to the beam, rusted and proud.

He moved to the side window, the one that had faced the sea. The pane was cracked. But it still opened.

And inside, just visible against the far wall — her cup.

The old steel tumbler she used for evening coffee. Still there. Still sitting by the shelf where she kept her prayer books, her worn comb, and the thread box missing its lid.

Vihaan didn't move.

He just stood there. One hand on the frame. The other resting against his chest, as though steadying a memory too tender to hold.

The breeze that drifted in smelled of rice, sea, and turmeric.

And maybe, just maybe, of her.

He sat down on the porch step, back against the pillar where he used to lean with his geometry textbook, pretending to study while secretly sketching boats.

And he let it come.

The remembering.

The ache.

The gratitude.

Not loud. Not tearful.

Just full.

Because this house wasn't a building.

It was the first thing that ever believed in him.

The next morning, before the sun had fully bloomed, Vihaan returned to the school.

No ceremony. No goodbyes.

Just one last moment he needed for himself.

He sat across the lane, under a tamarind tree that once offered shade to students who had missed their bus. The early air was still cool, scented faintly with smoke from someone's kitchen fire and the distant sizzle of oil catching on dosa batter.

He opened his sketchbook.

No ruler. No reference.

Just memory and breath. And slowly, carefully, he began to draw the school gate.

Not perfectly.

The rust wasn't symmetrical.

The arch slanted slightly to the left.

The letters were uneven, like they, too, had learned resilience before grammar.

But it was true.

He shaded in the pebbled path that led up to it. Added the crooked bell that always rang two minutes too late. The corner of the banyan's roots curling into the edge of the page like a signature.

And then, just above the gate, he wrote:

Where I first learned to carry things taller than myself.

He closed the sketchbook gently. Ran his hand across the cover not to flatten the page, but to bless it.

This wasn't just where he came from.

It was the place that had quietly built the scaffolding of who he had become.

And for the first time in years, Vihaan didn't feel like he was leaving something behind.

He felt like he was finally bringing it with him.

CHAPTER SIXTEEN

WHEN FRIENDS BECOME SHELTER

The signs were small at first.

A missed breakfast.

A skipped class.

A joke Nikhil didn't finish.

At IIT, no one questioned distance everyone wore exhaustion like a second skin. Lateness, messiness, the occasional "bro, I'm done" were part of the student dialect. But Vihaan... noticed rhythm. Not words.

And Nikhil's rhythm was off.

He laughed, sure. Still played cards late into the night. Still teased Aayush over his crush on the sociology girl and debated football with the same unnecessary intensity. But something in his laughter felt borrowed. A half-second too quick. A little too hollow at the edges.

And when he left the mess one evening without finishing his plate Vihaan knew.

Something was wrong.

He didn't ask.

Didn't press.

But he began paying attention.

Not with interrogation.

With presence.

He started saving a seat beside him in class, even when Nikhil didn't show. He brought back extra puris from the mess and left them by his desk without a note. He watched, gently, as the walls around his friend rose higher and knew that sometimes, walls weren't built out of pride, but panic.

One night, around 9:30, Vihaan saw him climb the stairs to the rooftop.

No books. No phone.

Just a hoodie and silence.

Vihaan followed, five minutes later.

Not to ask.

Not to fix.

Just... to sit.

The night air was crisp, the sky stained with orange light from the city, stars drowned by the glow of movement that never slept.

Nikhil was standing near the edge, looking out at the trees that bordered the hostel, arms crossed.

Vihaan sat down a few feet away. Cross-legged. Didn't say a word. The silence between them stretched like a quiet bridge.

No tension.

Just... waiting.

Eventually, Nikhil sat too.

Still no words

But something in the stillness softened.

Vihaan reached into his hoodie pocket, pulled out a single boiled candy the orange kind that tasted faintly of tamarind and childhood and slid it across the concrete between them.

Nikhil looked at it.

Then him.

Took it.

Unwrapped it slowly.

And whispered, "Thanks."

No context.

No explanation.

But Vihaan just nodded, as if to say: You don't have to tell me yet. But I'm here when you do.

The kind of friendship that doesn't need translation.

Only space.

The wind picked up.

Not the kind that howled or snapped laundry off wires just enough to ruffle hoodies, make hair move like thoughts.

They sat side by side now, legs stretched out across the cold rooftop, the tamarind candy between them gone.

Neither had spoken in five minutes.

It wasn't awkward.

Just quiet the kind of quiet you earn.

Finally, Nikhil exhaled. Not dramatically. Just... longer than usual. "I thought I'd be the one holding it together," he said softly. "Always figured... you know, I'm the loud one, the joke guy, the chill one."

Vihaan turned slightly, but said nothing.

Nikhil looked down at his hands, fingers fidgeting with the candy wrapper.

"My dad lost his job last month," he said, eyes fixed on a crack in the concrete. "Didn't tell anyone. Not even my mom at first. Thought it was temporary."

Vihaan stayed still. Listening. But present.

"I found out because Amma called me crying when the rent bounced," Nikhil added, voice barely audible now. "She asked if I could send money."

He chuckled bitter, hollow. "Me. The idiot who blew 400 bucks on momo night and forgot about his own phone bill."

Vihaan didn't flinch.

Didn't say, "It's okay."

Didn't say, "You'll figure it out."

He just looked at him.

And said, "I'm glad you told me."

Nikhil blinked.

And for a second a flicker only visible if you knew him well his face softened. The bravado fell. The weight showed.

"I just needed someone not to joke," he whispered.

Vihaan nodded. "Then I'll be that."

Silence again.

This time, warm.

Nikhil leaned back on his elbows, eyes scanning the sky. "You're weird, man. You don't say much, but you make it hard to lie."

Vihaan half-smiled. "That's probably because I grew up with Aachi." Nikhil laughed not loudly, but real. The kind that cracks open grief just enough to let something kinder in.

They sat there a while longer. Talking, eventually. Not just about his dad, but about fear. About pressure. About the quiet shame of pretending to be fine when you're not.

And when they finally stood, brushing dust from their jeans, the world below them felt a little less heavy.

Because sometimes, you don't need fixing.

You just need a person who stays.

Later that night, Vihaan sat on his bed with the lights off.

The corridor outside buzzed faintly someone boiling Maggi in the mess kitchen, the hum of a water purifier switching on, laughter from a room two doors down. Hostel life, alive as always.

But inside Vihaan's room, there was stillness.

Not emptiness.

Not loneliness.

Just a space where something meaningful had been made. Quietly. Carefully.

He reached into the side pocket of his bag and pulled out his sketchbook not to draw, but to hold it. The way one might hold a letter they hadn't opened yet, already knowing what it would say.

He thought about what Nikhil had whispered.

"I just needed someone not to joke."

It repeated itself, slow and steady, like the tide lapping at the shore near his old home.

And Vihaan realized that's what Aachi had always done for him.

She never filled his silences.

She sat beside them, cup of coffee in hand, listening to things he didn't yet know how to say.

He had thought of strength as something loud once something spoken, something seen.

But tonight, it felt like strength was just... presence.

It was knowing how to sit beside someone who's unraveling and not reach for the thread but simply say, "I'm here when you're ready to tie it back."

And that changed something in him.

He looked around his small, cluttered room the crumpled notes, the extra toothbrush someone had once left behind, the shoes lined up by the door that didn't quite close anymore.

And he felt something gentle settle in his chest.

Not pride.

Not burden.

Belonging.

He didn't need to be the top of the class.

Didn't need to make the room laugh.

He just needed to be someone people felt safe around.

And slowly, almost shyly, Vihaan smiled to himself in the dark.

Not because someone told him he mattered.

But because he finally believed he did.

It appeared beneath his sketchbook.

No envelope. No name.

Just a folded square of lined paper, slipped between pages of his site mechanics notebook the kind of paper used for quick calculations or forgotten shopping lists. But this one had weight.

Vihaan found it two days after the rooftop.

He'd been searching for a diagram on cantilever moments when the note tumbled out, brushed against his thigh, and landed on the floor with a softness that felt intentional.

He picked it up, turned it over.

The handwriting was familiar slanted, clean, no loops.

Meera.

"Even the strongest bridges need time to rest."

You're not the one everyone leans on because you're unbreakable.

It's because you don't run when they do.

That's beautiful. But don't forget to sit sometimes.

— M.

He didn't move for a long time after reading it.

Didn't fold it.

Didn't reread it.

Just held it in his hands, like something sacred.

There was no pressure in the words. No hint of expectation. Only a kind of recognition as if she'd seen the small invisible cost of being the person everyone turns to. And instead of thanking him for it, she simply said: I see you.

Vihaan leaned back against his chair and let the afternoon sun warm his legs through the window.

He thought of bridges.

Of tension.

Of weight.

Of how even the most elegant structures relied on the parts no one ever noticed the bolts, the bearings, the foundations built beneath the surface.

And maybe that was him.

Not the tallest.

Not the flashiest.

But quietly holding up what he could, day after day.

And maybe that was enough.

He tucked Meera's note back into the sketchbook not like a keepsake.

But like a message he'd someday need again.

The rain came suddenly.

One of those unseasonal Mumbai showers that had no regard for forecasts or umbrellas. Just clouds rolling in like moody percussion, then water thick and fast, drumming rooftops, flooding sidewalks, scattering people like leaves in wind.

It was just past 7 PM. Vihaan had just finished a long lab session and was crossing the hostel corridor when he spotted Aayush standing in the stairwell.

No phone.

No towel.

Just standing there, his back to the wall, watching the rain fall through the grating like it was trying to explain something.

His posture was different.

No music humming through his headphones. No dramatic poses. No "bro" flung casually like punctuation.

Just stillness.

Vihaan stopped.

"Aayush?"

No answer.

He stepped closer.

"I got my results," Aayush said, not turning around. "I failed the module."

Silence.

Vihaan waited.

"I thought I was safe. Just enough to scrape by, you know? But... I missed one quiz when I was sick, and the other one I bombed."

Another pause.

"I didn't even tell my parents I was struggling. Told them everything was chill."

His voice cracked slightly on that last word. Chill.

Vihaan stepped into the rain.

Didn't ask for more.

Didn't say "It's okay" or "We'll figure it out."

He just walked until he stood next to Aayush, under the downpour. Shoulder to shoulder.

Aayush looked at him, finally. Water streaked down his face maybe rain, maybe something else. He chuckled bitterly.

"You're nuts, man. You didn't even get wet when we played Holi but now you're just... what? Standing here like this?"

Vihaan shrugged. "Didn't feel right to carry an umbrella."

That cracked something open.

Aayush laughed. A real, tired, wet laugh. The kind that tastes like salt and relief.

They didn't go inside.

They stood in the rain until their shirts clung and the water pooled around their ankles and the city smelled like soaked earth and second chances.

And somewhere in that soaking silence, Aayush said:

"Thanks, da."

It didn't sound small.

It sounded like I was about to fall, and you didn't catch me you just stood beside me until I could stand again.

The mess was nearly empty.

Rain had pushed most students back into their rooms under blankets, behind laptops, wrapped in the lazy safety that only stormy nights could offer.

But at one corner table by the window, four cups of chai sat steaming in a quiet row.

Vihaan brought them, without asking.

No dramatic gesture. No "I got this."

Just a tray balanced carefully, fingers still damp from the rain, and a faint smile on his lips that said: sit, breathe, be.

Nikhil took his cup with a nod.

Aayush muttered something about finally warming up, eyes softer than usual.

Meera didn't say anything at all just looked at Vihaan, the way someone might look at a candle lit during a power cut. Not amazed. Just thankful it's there.

They didn't talk much.

Just sipped.

Outside, rain tapped against the glass. The smell of soaked earth drifted in. A dog barked twice in the distance, and someone somewhere was playing a radio old Hindi songs blurred by static.

Aayush nudged Vihaan gently. "You're such a... strange guy, da. Like, emotionally literate or something."

Vihaan raised an eyebrow. "That's your compliment?"

"Hey, I'm trying," Aayush grinned. "Shut up and drink your philosopher chai."

They all laughed the kind of laughter that doesn't echo, but settles. Meera reached for the napkin and drew a tiny cup with a smiley face on it. Passed it to Vihaan wordlessly.

He folded it once. Slipped it into his pocket like a keepsake.

And for the first time in a long while, none of them felt the weight of performance.

No one was being smart, or charming, or strong.

They were just being.

Together.

The corridor was dim as they walked back.

Vihaan carried the empty tray. Meera walked beside him, arms crossed over her notebook, her pace matched to his.

Neither of them spoke.

It wasn't the silence of awkwardness.

It was the kind of silence that follows care like the hush in a room after a baby falls asleep. Like the wind settling after a storm.

They reached the stairwell where their paths split.

She turned to him, paused.

"You know," she said, her voice soft but certain, "you don't talk much." Vihaan glanced at her, smiled faintly. "I know."

"But when you're around," she continued, "the world calms down."

He blinked.

She looked at him for a second longer then added, almost as if it wasn't meant to be said out loud:

"You make people feel safe."

Vihaan didn't answer.

Didn't know how.

Because what do you say to something that doesn't feel like a compliment, but like a truth you'd never had the words for before?

So he just nodded.

Not because he understood.

But because he hoped in some quiet way to be that for her, too. Meera didn't wait for him to reply.

She just smiled soft, crooked, fleeting and walked up the stairs, disappearing around the turn.

Vihaan stood there a moment longer.

The corridor light flickered once.

Rain tapped lightly against the hostel windows.

Somewhere, the world continued.

But inside him, something had settled.

He didn't feel proud.

He felt... real.

And maybe that was more important than anything else.

CHAPTER SEVENTEEN

THE ROOM YOU CARRY WITH YOU

She was sitting on the porch.

The sky behind her was grey not the kind that threatens rain, but the kind that softens the edges of memory. Everything was washed in light that looked like it had come from inside her, not the sun.

She was humming.

The same tune she used to hum while untangling flower garlands, her fingers moving like they were stitching the air into something sacred.

Vihaan didn't speak.

He stood barefoot on the edge of the step, just like he did every morning before leaving for school. Her steel tumbler sat by her feet, half-full. Jasmine petals curled at the hem of her sari like punctuation.

She looked at him. Not smiled just looked. Like she'd been waiting.

And then she said, in the voice he hadn't heard since that morning on the platform:

"Even silence has soil, kanna.

Plant something in it."

Vihaan blinked.

And woke. It was still dark.

The hostel room was hushed the kind of hush that comes before the city remembers it must be noisy again.

He sat up slowly, the dream still clinging to him like the smell of roasted cumin faint, comforting, impossible to forget.

His breath felt uneven.

Not panicked. Not sad.

Just... stirred.

He touched his palm to his chest, half-expecting to feel the weight of her words pressed there like jasmine strands.

But there was only skin.

Warm.

And waiting.

He looked at his desk.

Papers. Pens. Sketchbooks.

And suddenly, he felt it the absence that wasn't a void, but a presence with edges. Like an unfinished room. One he'd walked past every day without knowing it needed to be built.

That morning, as the sun began peeling gold across the window grills, Vihaan wrote a single sentence in his notebook:

Some dreams aren't messages.

They're invitations.

And for the first time in months, he whispered her name out loud.

Not like a wish.

But like a foundation.

He didn't mean to choose the corner.

It chose him.

There was nothing special about it just the square of space between his desk and the window grill, where the afternoon sun poured in like quiet tea. A patch of cracked tile where his backpack usually slouched, where his slippers always ended up sideways, forgotten.

But that morning, after the dream, Vihaan moved the bag.

And for the first time, he looked at that corner like it had been waiting.

Waiting to be noticed.

To be used.

To be named.

He swept it clean not with a broom, but with his hand, brushing away chalk dust and two tiny moth wings like someone clearing space on the floor for a prayer mat.

Then he gathered three things:

A small square of white cotton cloth.

A copper tumbler he'd once used for hostel haldi milk.

And a single spiral-bound notebook, weathered at the spine.

He placed them down with care.

No incense. No photos.

Just space.

He folded the cloth into a neat square, set the tumbler gently in its center, and placed the notebook beside it. Inside that notebook were half-formed poems, fragments of letters never sent, and a sketch he'd once started of Aachi's feet as she sat threading jasmine.

He didn't speak.

Didn't label it.

But he knew this was her room now. Here, in the place between concrete and sunlight, she would live again.

Not as a ghost.

But as memory with breath.

When Nikhil barged in later, ranting about misplaced USB drives, he paused mid-sentence when he saw it.

"New project?" he asked.

Vihaan shook his head.

Just smiled.

"Old one," he said softly. "I just never finished building it."

The pencil felt heavier that evening.

Not because it was new it wasn't.

It was worn down, chewed slightly at the end, and smudged with the residue of forgotten diagrams.

But tonight, it wasn't for beam analysis.

It was for her.

Vihaan sat cross-legged in front of his tiny corner by the window, sketchbook balanced on his thigh. Outside, the hostel was alive with life laughter echoing from down the hall, the dull thud of a cricket ball somewhere near the mess, the evening birds making negotiations in the banyan trees.

But inside his room, everything was still.

He closed his eyes.

And tried to remember the shape of her hands.

Not her face. Not her voice.

Just... the hands.

The way her fingers moved when tying jasmine threads, looping each blossom with a tenderness that felt like scripture.

The fine lines around her knuckles, worn from decades of sweeping verandas and grinding masalas with a stone.

The mole near her thumb that he used to trace with his pinky as a child, believing it held magic.

And slowly, the pencil moved.

Not with technique. Not for perfection.

But with devotion.

He didn't erase. Didn't refine.

Just let the hand form on paper the way it lived in memory imperfect, beautiful, alive.

It took him twenty minutes.

When he was done, he looked at it and felt something flutter inside him.

Not grief.

Not ache.

Warmth.

Because the drawing wasn't just hers.

It was his the version of her he had carried silently for so long, finally given shape.

He placed the sketch beside the tumbler in the corner, anchoring it under a folded paperweight Meera had once made in a workshop a small square of concrete with a crack through the center.

Vihaan looked at it.

And whispered, "You built everything I love."

It began on a Sunday.

Not because he planned it, or marked his calendar with intention.

But because the air felt slower that morning, and the sun slipped in through the curtains like it was knocking instead of barging in.

He brewed tea.

Not hostel tea not the sugary, hurried liquid passed in dented steel tumblers.

This was his recipe. Aachi's.

He had carried the memory of it in muscle more than in mind. A rhythm. A ritual.

Boil water. Add grated ginger. One crushed cardamom pod. A pinch of jaggery. Milk last always last, so the colour shifts like dusk on the sea.

He poured it into the copper tumbler he'd placed in the corner.

And beside it, he laid a single jasmine flower. It wasn't fresh he'd bought it from the campus vendor the night before, slightly wilted at the edges.

But it was enough.

He didn't say anything.

Just sat across from it, back against the bedframe, tea cooling between them like a conversation that didn't need words.

There was no prayer.

No chant.

Just breath.

And a sense that in this act in the making and placing and pausing he had somehow told her, I remember you.

He finished the tea. Carefully folded the cloth. Replaced the flower with a new one from the bundle he now kept wrapped in damp paper in his drawer.

And just before standing up, he whispered:

"Next Sunday. Same time. You better show up."

And somehow, in the stillness of the room

he felt like she did.

It took him a week to begin.

The paper was cream-colored, with faint blue lines. The kind his school once used for essay tests. He found it folded between two textbooks, slightly yellowed, smelling faintly of dust and turmeric. He sharpened his pencil. Not for clarity but out of respect.

And then, without planning, he began to write.

> "*Aachi,*
>
> *I'm doing fine. Not great, not terrible. Just somewhere in between. Like the light in the corridor when it's not quite morning but not night either.*
>
> *I made your tea last Sunday. Not exactly right I forgot the cloves. But I remembered the jaggery, and how you always stirred it counterclockwise, as if sweetness had a direction.*
>
> *Sometimes I think of your hands, and I can still feel the pressure of your fingers tapping the back of mine three times, always three. You never said what it meant. I think you knew I'd figure it out someday.*
>
> *I keep trying to build things that last.*
>
> *I don't know if I'm good at it yet.*
>
> *But I remember what you said before I left — about not forgetting where I'm from.*
>
> *I think I used to think "home" was the house. The sea. The swing. But now I think... Home is the part of me that still sounds like you when I talk to someone I love.*
>
> *I miss you. Every day.*
>
> *But I also carry you. And I hope that's enough.*
>
> *Love,*
>
> *Vihaan*"

He folded it gently, no creases. Tied it with a thin piece of thread. And placed it in a small steel box beneath his bed the one that once held nails, rubber bands, old receipts.

It didn't need a lock.

Just memory.

And the quiet, sacred promise:

You are not gone. You are just elsewhere.

And I will write you again.

She didn't ask about the corner.

Didn't comment on the copper tumbler. Didn't question the folded cloth or the way the space near his desk always smelled faintly of ginger tea and wilted jasmine.

She just... noticed.

It was a Wednesday when she came by to return a shared lab journal. She stepped into the room, paused at the doorway, and looked not at the books, not at the diagrams pinned to his corkboard but at that small, curated corner of stillness.

Vihaan watched her eyes land there.

Saw the flicker of understanding pass across her face. Not confusion. Not pity. Just recognition. She didn't ask. Didn't need to.

She handed him the book, made some passing joke about Aayush's handwriting, and left.

And Vihaan thought that was the end of it.

But the next Sunday morning, when he returned from a walk to the chai stall, he saw it.

A second flower.

Placed beside the tumbler.

Fresher than the one he'd left. Whiter. Still carrying dew at the edges like it had only just left its stem.

No note. No initials.

Just presence.

He didn't move it.

Didn't touch it.

He sat down beside the corner and sipped his tea, letting the weight of that second flower settle in beside him not as intrusion, but as invitation.

And for the first time in his ritual, he didn't feel alone.

He felt joined.

Quietly. Kindly.

Not in mourning.

But in remembrance made communal.

It was just after midnight when he opened the sketchbook.

Not the one with beams and soil maps.

The other one the one with loose corners and tea stains, with fragments of poetry and the folded jasmine from two Sundays ago pressed between the back pages.

The air in the room was quiet. The fan spun with a hum soft enough to disappear into thought.

Vihaan sat cross-legged on his bed, pencil in hand.

He hadn't planned to write.

But something inside him felt... complete. Not in the way you finish a project. In the way you realize you don't have to finish healing to feel whole.

He flipped to the next blank page.

Paused.

And wrote:

"Some structures aren't made of concrete.

They're made of memory.

Of tea steam and jasmine stems.

Of hands that taught you how to sweep the floor and sit with silence.

Of voices that still echo when you do something right, and when you do something wrong.

They are not built once. They are carried.

And if you're lucky they hold you back together when the world forgets your name."

He stared at the words.

Not because he doubted them.

But because they felt true.

Not in a textbook sense.

In a home sense.

He closed the book gently.

Turned off the light.

And lay back, arms behind his head, listening to the fan. To the quiet. To the way something tender now lived where the ache used to sit.

The room was still small.

But it held more than before.

And Vihaan for the first time in a long time felt held.

CHAPTER EIGHTEEN

THE FOUNDATIONS YOU NEVER SEE

The day began the way it always did.

Light spilled across the corridor in long, golden lines, catching motes of dust in its path like tiny fireflies. Doors creaked open one by one. Buckets scraped against bathroom tiles. Slippers slapped across cool floors.

And Vihaan was already up.

He moved through the quiet in that familiar, deliberate way not rushed, not slow. Like someone who believed the world deserved a gentle entrance.

He filled his bottle from the mess filter, left it near the door for Aayush, who always forgot. Slipped a Post-it note on Nikhil's desk that read, "You didn't leave your charger. I just wanted to remind you you didn't." (He had, of course. And he'd smile when he read it.)

Vihaan carried an old wrench in his back pocket not for drama, but because the chai vendor outside the back gate had a cart wheel that stuck. Every few mornings, it needed coaxing, and Vihaan had a way of fixing things without asking questions.

He didn't speak much on his rounds.

Just nodded. Held doors. Picked up the fallen badminton shuttle without breaking stride. Pulled up a mess bench slightly out of place. And no one really noticed.

That's the beauty of invisible kindness. It doesn't shine.

It settles.

As he walked past the banyan tree by the admin block, a small girl from the staff quarters — maybe six, maybe seven — waved shyly from her perch on the low wall.

Vihaan stopped. Fished a red jelly from his pocket soft, wrapped in gold foil and held it out wordlessly.

Her face bloomed into the kind of smile you wanted to remember forever.

He walked on, thinking about the kind of bridges that didn't span rivers or highways but mornings like these.

Tiny, unnoticed spans between people.

Built in silence.

Held with care.

They never said it out loud, but people noticed.

The boy from Room 103 who started leaving extra bookmarks in the library's most borrowed textbooks? He'd once found a post-it on his door from an unknown classmate that simply read: "Page 34. Don't skip it. It might change your life."

He still had that note.

The chai vendor outside the main gate the one with the crooked cart started giving a second cup free to any student who looked like they hadn't slept. When asked why, he just smiled and said, "Because someone once fixed my wheel without asking."

And in the E-block women's hostel, a small handmade flyer appeared on the board one morning:

"Need a break from exams? Come paint a wall with us."

No club name. No sign-up sheet. Just a time and place.

It drew fifteen students. Someone brought music. Someone else brought lemon soda. The wall became a collage of colors and languages.

At the bottom, someone painted:

"Kindness is structural. You may not see it, but you feel it."

No one connected it to Vihaan.

But it didn't matter.

Because he never did these things to be seen.

He did them because he saw.

And sometimes, that's all it takes one person to pay attention. To quietly fill the cracks where no one else is looking.

The world didn't shift with applause.

It shifted with alignment.

That evening, Aayush bumped into a first-year who'd been crying in the library. No spectacle. No drama.

He just sat beside her.

And said, "You know... Vihaan once told me that failing a test isn't failing at life. I believed him. You should too."

She nodded.

Neither of them knew that Vihaan was, at that moment, fixing a leaking pipe near the sports block alone, quiet, content.

Not realizing the size of the bridge he'd become.

It was Meera who dragged him there.

"Ten minutes," she'd said. "If it's boring, we'll sneak out and split a samosa."

Vihaan had raised an eyebrow. "You hate public events."

"I hate loud ones," she replied. "But this one's quiet. Open mic. No mics."

They sat near the back of the rec hall, backs against the cool wall, knees brushing in silence.

A few string lights framed the modest stage. No banner. No posters. Just a group of students seated cross-legged on mattresses, waiting their turn.

The theme, someone whispered near the entrance, was:

"Someone who changed something for you without knowing it."

The stories began.

A girl from architecture spoke about a stranger who left a bar of chocolate and a sticky note during midterms: "You're not invisible. Just quiet. That's different."

A boy from metallurgy shared how, during his worst semester, someone anonymously paid his mess dues.

A junior talked about a small hand-written quote she found in the bathroom: "You are more than your lowest grade." She'd copied it into her diary and read it every exam season since.

And slowly, Vihaan's breath caught in his throat.

Not because they named him.

They never did.

But in every story in every small act of kindness, every wordless gesture, every quiet moment that softened someone's world he heard shadows of himself.

Like someone had taken pieces of his heart and left them, unknowingly, in other people's pockets.

And now those pieces were speaking back.

By the time the sixth story ended, Vihaan couldn't meet Meera's gaze.

She didn't look at him either.

She just reached down, slipped a piece of paper into his hand folded twice, jasmine-scented.

On it, one line:

"The strongest bridges don't ask to be crossed. They just wait."

Vihaan looked up at the ceiling, where the string lights blurred into stars.

He didn't cry.

But something inside him... bowed.

Not from weight.

From recognition.

It was tucked into the back of his sketchbook.

He found it days after the event not while searching, but while absentmindedly flipping pages between classes. The note was folded clean, the edges soft like it had been carried in someone's pocket for a while.

No name.

Just four short lines, in delicate pen:

"*You changed everything.*

You never asked for attention.

You just showed up.
And now I do too. "

Vihaan stared at it for a long time.

His fingers brushed the paper as if it were too sacred to unfold all at once. It wasn't the kind of note that demanded explanation. It didn't even want a reply.

It was the echo of something he hadn't realized he'd sung.

He didn't know who wrote it.

Maybe the girl who cried on the library stairs.

Maybe the boy from the mess who always had an extra spoon.

Maybe someone he passed every day without seeing but who saw him anyway.

It didn't matter.

Because the words did something to him.

They held him.

Not as a hero.

Not as a fixer.

But as a foundation.

Something that steadied people even when they didn't know what they were building yet.

That night, he didn't journal.

He just folded the note again.

Slipped it into his wallet.

And sat beside his corner ritual — jasmine, tea, her hands letting the words curl quietly around him like warmth in a room with no heater.

It didn't feel like closure.

It felt like a beginning.

Because kindness doesn't retire.

It recycles.

It was late. The kind of late where even the night had begun to loosen its hold, letting in soft tremors of dawn through the hostel window panes.

Meera knocked once.

Vihaan looked up from his desk, sketchbook open, pen idle.

She didn't step in right away. Just lingered in the doorway like she wasn't sure if what she wanted to say would fit inside the room.

"You ever think," she began, voice low, "that some people build without ever laying bricks?"

Vihaan tilted his head slightly. "You're speaking in metaphors again."

She walked in, arms folded. There was no notebook this time. No teasing remark.

Just her. And something tender in her silence.

"I watched you," she said. "Not just this week. Since the beginning." He didn't interrupt.

"You walk like someone who believes no one's watching. But you move like someone who hopes someone will feel better just because you passed by."

She sat down on the edge of the bed, beside the window.

"You fix broken taps, you carry plates that aren't yours, you leave people little pieces of peace without ever naming it. And the thing is..."

She looked up, eyes meeting his.

"Not all builders use cement, Vihaan."

He blinked. The lump in his throat didn't ask for attention, but it rose anyway.

"You... build people. Quietly. Lovingly. And you never ask if they noticed. That's rare. That's—"

"Enough," he said gently, smiling to stop the flood.

Meera nodded. "Okay."

She stood up. Walked to the door. Then paused.

"You don't need applause," she said. "But it would be criminal not to say this at least once."

Vihaan waited.

She turned back, softened. "You make this place feel more like home."

And then she left.

No fireworks.

No music.

Just footprints on the corridor tile, and the sound of someone who had, perhaps for the first time, been fully named.

Vihaan turned back to his sketchbook.

On a blank page, he wrote just two words:

"*Invisible infrastructure.*"

And below it, a sentence:

"*If they feel safe, I've built enough.*"

CHAPTER NINETEEN

THE LAST ROOM, THE FIRST WINDOW

It was the small drawer under his desk.

The one that never opened all the way unless you jiggled it sideways first. The one that swallowed coins, pens, tiny wrappers, and pieces of four years he hadn't thought to keep but had.

Vihaan knelt beside it, the early morning light seeping in through the curtains, soft as breath. He wrapped his fingers around the rusted handle and pulled.

The drawer groaned.

Of course it did.

It always sounded like it was tired too like it had seen enough latenight assignments, spilled coffee, and crumpled frustration to demand retirement.

Inside:

A broken protractor.

A mess bill folded eight times, with a tiny note from Aayush scrawled on the back: "You owe me samosa interest."

An unused thank-you card.

Half a dried jasmine flower.

He touched each thing like it might speak.

There was a paper crane from Nikhil's attempt to teach him origami during their second semester. Vihaan had failed miserably. This was the only one he didn't crush. He remembered Nikhil saying, "This one's got character. Kinda like you. All angles. No symmetry. But somehow standing."

He smiled.

There was a key to a locker he hadn't used since second year. A sketch of a stairwell Meera once said reminded her of a poem he couldn't remember which one. And beneath it all, a receipt from a field trip to a bridge site he barely paid attention to back when engineering still felt like a course and not a language.

Vihaan didn't cry.

But his chest ached not with sadness, but with a kind of reverence. This drawer had become a reliquary.

Not of achievement.

But of presence.

He found the charger he thought he'd lost. A pen that still worked.

The old wrench he used to fix the chai cart. And at the very back a steel paperclip, bent into the shape of a heart. No idea when. Or why.

He placed it all on the bed, sorting things into piles: keep, discard, maybe.

The "maybe" pile grew fastest.

Because how do you decide what pieces of your life deserve a suitcase?

How do you pack a self you don't want to leave behind?

He sat back, exhaled, and whispered to the drawer:

"Thanks for holding me, when I didn't know what I was even becoming."

Then he closed it.

Slowly.

Carefully.

Like it was a chapter.

Not of things.

But of himself.

The window wasn't special.

Just two metal panes that stuck in the monsoons, with rust along the bottom rail and a lone sticker someone had left behind years ago: "IITians eat stress for breakfast."

Vihaan had tried peeling it once. It wouldn't come off.

But this window cracked frame and all had been his first introduction to the city.

Back then, it had felt like a screen between him and the world beyond. He used to sit behind it with a textbook open and a mind too loud to read. The road outside had seemed like another country. Foreign. Fast. Unreachable.

Now, he sat with the same city in view.

But it felt... smaller.

Not because it had changed.

Because he had grown.

He rested his arms on the sill.

Watched a few students running, late for something that probably didn't matter as much as they thought. A dog trotted beside a cycle. A chai vendor opened his stall and began boiling water. Everything was as it always had been.

But Vihaan watched it like someone watching a film where he'd once played a minor role... and was now reading the script as the narrator.

He thought of the boy who had first walked into this room four years ago, suitcase too full, voice too small, eyes still searching for sea.

And then he thought of this boy.

This man.

The one who had loved quietly.

Who had failed, forgiven.

Who had learned not just how to build with concrete but how to hold people together with silence and care.

A butterfly floated past the window.

And he wondered not for the first time if he'd somehow become the very thing Aachi hoped he would: not just successful, but kind.

He picked up a pencil from the sill.

On the back of an old assignment sheet, he wrote a sentence without thinking:

The window didn't change.

But I learned how to see.

He folded it and slipped it into his pocket.

Not because it mattered.

But because, somehow, it did.

He didn't take his phone.

Just his hands in his pockets and the quiet beneath his ribs.

The corridor still smelled faintly of damp socks and photocopied notes. A familiar mix of life and paper. Vihaan walked slowly, letting his fingers brush the cold railings, the worn paint, the places his palms had once gripped too tightly during moments of panic.

He passed the water cooler that had flooded twice in his second year the same one where Nikhil had poured water over his head during exams and said, "Hydration is salvation, bro."

He smiled.

The staircase still creaked on the third step.

The mess hall was almost empty. One staff auntie refilled the steel jugs like it was any other day. No finality. Just routine. That comforted him more than celebration ever could.

Vihaan walked to the corner table.

The one where Meera once sat with a cut on her hand, refusing help. The one where Aayush cried laughing into his biryani.

The one where Vihaan had once quietly left a note for a stranger who looked like they hadn't eaten in two days.

He didn't sit.

He just placed his hand flat on the tabletop not to take anything, but to leave something.

From there, he wandered to the terrace.

The place where Nikhil had told the truth about his father's job. Where the rain had once baptized Aayush's breakdown. Where they had all stood, arms open to the sky, when exams ended, shouting nothing in particular just releasing the year from their lungs.

It was empty now.

Except for the wind.

Vihaan stood at the edge and looked out not at the skyline, but at the air above it.

There were no flashbacks.

No montage.

Just the quiet truth: he had lived here.

He had grown here.

And the walls chipped and dusty as they were knew.

He ran his hand along the railing one last time, turned around, and whispered to the stairwell:

"Thank you for echoing me back when I didn't know who I was."

The bed was stripped bare.

Just the mattress now a little sunken in the middle, the edges curled like pages of a book left out in the rain. The sheet lay rumpled beside it, soft from too many washes, faintly carrying the scent of talcum and late nights.

Meera stood in the doorway.

No announcement. No knock. She was just there like always.

Vihaan looked up. "It's done."

She glanced at the empty shelves, the stacked books, the packed bags. "Not quite," she said. "Your folding skills are still criminal."

He smirked.

She stepped forward, picked up one end of the sheet. He took the other.

They stood at either side of the bed, lifting the cotton between them like a sail waiting for wind.

And then slowly, rhythmically they began to fold.

Corner to corner.

Edge to edge.

No words.

Just hands moving in sync.

A breath between gestures.

A stillness between years.

He remembered how they used to bicker over lab reports. How she once handed him a tea cup and said, "This is how you say sorry without saying it." How she once laughed so hard at his math joke that she dropped her lunch tray.

All of it lived here now folded into the silence between them.

On the final fold, their fingers touched.

Meera didn't move.

Neither did he.

And when they finally let go, the sheet was folded clean, square, warm from their hands.

She placed it at the foot of the bed. Looked up. Her eyes shone, not with tears but with something gentler. Something braver.

"Promise me something," she said.

He nodded.

"Don't become one of those people who forget what made them kind."

Vihaan swallowed. "Only if you promise something too."

She raised a brow.

"Keep making the world quieter. One jasmine at a time."

A pause.

A smile.

No hug. No handhold. Just her fingers brushing the doorway frame as she left like she was leaving a little part of herself behind.

And Vihaan stood there, beside the folded sheet, feeling like he'd just tucked a chapter into his chest.

Not closed.

Just... held.

The bed creaked beneath him as he sat.

The bags were zipped. The shelves empty. The walls bare. Even the sunlight looked softer now, as if it knew this would be its last dance across these tiles with him in the room.

Vihaan leaned back, arms resting on his knees.

And for the first time all day, he didn't do anything.

He just sat.

Letting the weight of the quiet press gently against his chest.

This was supposed to be the moment where he thought about engineering about his first design drawing, his first site visit, the exam that nearly broke him.

But his mind didn't go there.

It went to...

Aachi's voice calling "kanna" in the early morning light.

The broken chai cart that needed fixing more often than it didn't.

Aayush dancing on the mess table with samosas in both hands.

Meera placing a single jasmine beside his tea without saying a word.

Nikhil reading poetry to a wall at 2 a.m., and calling it therapy.

These weren't lessons.

They were truths.

Things he couldn't quote in a viva or submit on a term paper. But things that had shaped him far more than any classroom ever could.

He reached for his notebook.

Flipped past diagrams and equations. Past unit conversions and soil analysis.

And on a clean page, he wrote:

> *"I came here to learn how to build bridges.*
> *And somewhere along the way, I became one.*
> *Not of steel.*
> *Of small silences. Of tea cups. Of folded bedsheets. Of showing up even when no one asked."*

He tapped his pencil gently against the page, once, twice.

Then smiled.

Because in this moment with no one watching, no one grading he knew he had passed something far more important than a degree.

He had learned how to hold the world with care.

The switch clicked.

And the room dimmed into stillness.

Vihaan stood at the threshold, hand still resting on the light panel. The ceiling fan hummed its last spin above, fading into a whir that would soon become someone else's background noise.

He looked around once more.

The mattress was bare.

The desk, clean.

The window, half open letting in the faint scent of wet leaves and distant rain.

It looked like nothing now.

Just four walls, a fan, a view.

But he knew better.

This room had held his fear. His first all-nighter. His first note from someone who understood his silence. It had echoed with his laughter, absorbed his tears, held his rituals, and forgiven his messes.

It wasn't a room.

It was a witness.

And now, it stood empty.

But not hollow.

Because what it had built what they had built here was going with him.

Vihaan stepped out slowly.

Rolled the suitcase behind him with a sound like old film unwinding. Tugged the door shut, but didn't let it slam.

He paused just before it latched.

Whispered:

"Thank you for being the first place I was ever truly myself."

Then closed it.

Not with finality.

But with care.

And as he walked down the corridor past rooms buzzing with life he no longer belonged to he felt no loss.

Only fullness.

He didn't carry regret.
Or anxiety.
Or even hope.
He carried everything that mattered.
The kind of everything that weighs nothing.
The kind of everything you don't pack in bags.
Because it lives in your chest.
And keeps you warm long after the last room goes dark.

WHERE THE SEA MEETS THE SKY

The train curved gently into Mumbai just after sunrise the same arrival hour as five years ago.

But this time, Vihaan didn't press his face to the window. He sat back, elbows resting on his knees, eyes soft as the station rolled into view. The glass reflected his profile now older, a little sharper around the jaw, but still unmistakably him. Just... steadier.

He hadn't intended to take the train.

But something about returning that way along the same route, over the same bridges, through the same slow-breathing towns felt like a quiet vow kept.

Mumbai emerged from mist and metal.

The city hadn't changed much. It still pulsed like it had somewhere to be. Still smelled of hot pav and exhaust. Still filled every silence with possibility. But Vihaan saw it differently now.

Not as a stranger.

Not even as a visitor.

But as someone who once grew here.

He stepped off the train with no one to meet him.

No Aachi. No Meera. No anxious glances from first-year students or professors hurrying past with folders in hand. Just the low hum of morning Mumbai its people already halfway into their day.

Vihaan walked out of the station alone.

And didn't feel alone.

He hailed a taxi, his suitcase balanced on the edge of the seat. The driver asked, "Airport?"

Vihaan hesitated. Then shook his head.

"Marine Drive first."

The man nodded, wordless. As if he understood.

The city passed by in a blur of grey and gold.

Billboards for things he didn't need. People selling things he already carried. The chai vendor near campus still at his spot thinner now, older. A group of college students passed by, laughing about something that didn't matter but probably would to them for a long time.

Vihaan smiled.

He wasn't sentimental. He was grateful.

For every version of himself that had walked this city's spine the afraid boy, the open-hearted friend, the reluctant leader, the quiet builder.

They all still walked beside him.

Not left behind.

Just grown through.

He reached Marine Drive as the sun began its late-morning shimmer on the water.

The sea stretched out before him, as if it had been holding its breath for this very reunion. And in its low, constant rhythm, he heard Aachi again not as a voice, but as a presence:

"You are not leaving home, kanna.

You are extending it."

He took a slow breath.

The city moved behind him.

But the sea the sea waited.

And in the space between arrival and goodbye, Vihaan stood still.

He didn't visit a temple.

He didn't light a lamp or recite a prayer or kneel before a framed photograph with garlands and tears.

He just walked to the corner near a flower stall off Charni Road.

The same stall that used to sell loose jasmine strands in plastic trays.

The same aunty who once gave him an extra flower "for good luck" before an exam, as if the gods cared about cement ratios.

She wasn't there anymore.

A younger woman ran the stall now. Her bangles clinked softly as she sorted petals into piles. Vihaan picked a strand. Paid in exact change. And as he turned to leave, the woman called after him:

"Sir... this smells fresh today."

Vihaan nodded.

"It always did," he said.

He walked with the jasmine looped loosely around his fingers.

Didn't wear it. Didn't pocket it. Just held it like something worth remembering.

He passed a small tea stall, paused.

The man behind the counter looked up. "One cutting?"

Vihaan nodded.

The tea arrived in a glass that was chipped, still warm from the last pour. He cupped it between both palms and took the first sip.

It tasted wrong.

Too sweet. Too watery.

But somehow it healed.

He stood there for a long while. The sea on one side. The city on the other. Between them: the steam of the tea, the scent of jasmine, and a silence that spoke in his grandmother's voice.

He whispered, just once:

> *"I brought you with me.*
> *Not in my bag.*
> *In my spine.*
> *In my steps."*

He looked up at the sea, wide and bright, and thought of all the times Aachi had spoken of the ocean as if it were an old friend.

And now it felt like one.

Not because it was calm. But because it remembered.

He didn't cry.

He closed his eyes.

Let the jasmine slip into the wind. Let the last sip of tea roll down his throat.

And in that moment beneath the wide open sky and the restless sea Vihaan didn't feel alone.

He felt built.

By love.

By memory.

By her.

She was already there.

Seated at the far curve of the promenade, legs tucked beneath her, eyes on the horizon like she was listening to something only the sea could say.

Vihaan spotted her before she turned. Her hair caught in the breeze. A cloth tote bag rested by her feet, its handle looped through her fingers like she didn't want it to leave.

He didn't call out. Just walked slowly toward her, the jasmine still lingering on his skin, the taste of over-sweet tea warming his throat.

When he reached her, she didn't move.

Didn't say hi.

Didn't ask how the train was.

Just patted the space beside her, a small arc of granite that suddenly felt like the only place in the city made for him.

Vihaan sat.

The breeze curled around them.

Pigeons rustled along the edge. Couples leaned into one another down the stretch. Waves clapped the rocks in irregular applause.

"I thought you wouldn't come," she said softly.

"I almost didn't," he replied.

A beat passed.

"Why?"

He looked straight ahead. "Because goodbyes used to feel like erasing."

She nodded.

"And now?"

He turned to her. "Now they feel like... editing. You keep the best parts. You cut the noise."

Meera smiled that quiet, sideways smile that said she understood something deeper than the words themselves.

They didn't talk much.

Not at first.

They just sat.

Shoulders not touching, but not distant either.

Her fingers fidgeted with a tassel on her tote. His thumb ran over the edge of his ticket to London, folded neatly in his pocket.

And then, after a long silence the kind that only fits between people who've earned it Meera whispered:

"Do you ever feel like some people are made to leave, so that others can stay better?"

He thought about it.

Shook his head.

"I think some people leave... so the world doesn't forget how to carry softness."

She turned to him, eyes full.

And said nothing.

Because that was Vihaan.

He didn't pierce. He didn't overwhelm.

He stayed.

Even while preparing to go.

"Do you remember," she asked, her voice barely louder than the waves, "the first time we met?"

Vihaan tilted his head. "You were yelling at a printer."

She chuckled. "I was yelling at the power supply. The printer was innocent."

"You still printed upside-down."

She smiled, then let the silence return. The kind that didn't rush to be filled.

He leaned back, arms behind him on the concrete. The sea stretched out like an exhale too tired to come back in.

"I used to think I'd leave this place with big lessons," he said.

"And?" she asked.

"I'm leaving with small ones instead. The way jasmine smells different depending on the day. The way someone's silence can feel like safety. That kindness is... architectural."

She looked at him sideways. "Structural integrity."

"Exactly," he said. "The things that hold us up even when we don't know they're there."

Another pause.

The ocean kissed the rocks. Someone's radio played an old Hindi song in the distance.

"I thought I had to do something big to matter," Meera said. "To prove I deserved the dreams I carried."

Vihaan turned to her. "You never needed proof. You just needed space."

She met his gaze.

And there it was again that softness between them. That ease. That knowing.

No promises.

No declarations.

Just a shared acknowledgment: I see you. I've always seen you.

They sat like that for a long time.

Not measuring the time.

Not fearing its end.

When a cool gust of wind lifted a strand of her hair into his eyes, she didn't push it back.

And when it settled, he simply whispered:

"Thank you. For never trying to fix me. Just for sitting beside me while I found the shape of who I was."

She nodded.

Eyes on the sea.

Smile on her lips.

Love not spoken, but present.

Like a poem that didn't rhyme.

But made you feel more than words ever could.

The sky had begun to soften that liminal blue where the sun doesn't set all at once, but tucks itself away inch by inch like it's reluctant to leave.

Vihaan stood, brushing sea dust from his jeans. His suitcase handle clicked upright. The wind played with the hem of his shirt.

He looked down at Meera.

She hadn't moved.

Still sitting, still watching the waves as if they might spell something out. A language only she could translate.

Then she looked up and said, simply:

"You look lighter."

He exhaled.

"Maybe because I finally packed the right things."

Meera stood too.

There was a pause between them. Not hesitation just tenderness stretching its limbs one last time.

She reached for his wrist.

Not his hand.

Not his shoulder.

Just that small part where the pulse beats quietly proof of life, and something deeper.

"You carry her well," she said.

Vihaan nodded.

"She taught me how," he whispered. "Without words."

Their eyes met, not with intensity, but with that gentle recognition only two old souls can share. The kind of connection that isn't afraid of goodbyes, because it trusts continuity more than closeness.

Meera didn't cry.

She didn't say I'll miss you.

She said:

"Walk gently, Vihaan."

He smiled.

"You too, Meera."

And with that, he turned the sea behind him, the sky ahead and began to walk.

Each step was quiet.

But none of them felt alone.

The promenade curved gently toward the edge of the sea that familiar spot where the city seemed to dissolve into light.

Vihaan walked slowly.

Each step was soft, but certain.

His suitcase trailed behind him with a faint rhythm, like the tail end of a song only he could hear. The sounds of the city thinned honks, chatter, street dogs barking until all that remained was the hush of waves and the hush within him.

He paused at the far edge.

The sea stretched out like a breath held just a second longer than usual. The horizon blurred into the sky no line, no division. Just blue folding into blue.

He stood there for a long moment.

Not thinking.

Not remembering.

Just being.

He reached into his pocket and pulled out a folded scrap of paper a quote he had once scribbled in a lecture he hadn't been listening to:

"Maybe we don't arrive at new places.

Maybe we just finally recognize we've been walking toward ourselves all along."

He read it once.

Then let it go.

The wind caught it.

Lifted it.

Didn't tear it — just carried it.

And Vihaan smiled.
Not because anything had been resolved.
But because he finally understood —
Home wasn't behind him.
It wasn't ahead of him.
It was beneath his skin.
In the way he poured tea.
In the way he folded his bedsheet.
In the way he said someone's name like a gift, not a sound.
He looked at the water one last time.
Not to say goodbye.
But to say:
"I'm ready."
Then he turned.
And walked toward the sky.

Epilogue

He hadn't chosen the window seat.

It had been assigned.

But when he sat down, and the cabin filled with the soft thuds of closing compartments and the rustle of safety cards, Vihaan felt... strangely placed. As if the sky had kept a seat warm for him, knowing he'd be on this flight long before he booked it.

The engine thrummed beneath him a low vibration, like a distant heartbeat.

The kind Aachi used to hum when she stirred rasam: constant, even, full of comfort.

He looked out.

The tarmac glistened with leftover rain.

Runway lights blinked like slow eyelids.

A lone bird paused on the edge of a taxiing path, as if unsure whether to fly or watch him go.

And then motion.

The wheels lifted from the earth.

Not in a rush. Not with fear.

Just faithfully.

His chest didn't tighten. His breath didn't hitch.

He simply watched the city fold into patchwork streets becoming strings, buildings turning to paper silhouettes.

Mumbai receded.

But it didn't vanish.

It layered itself into him, gently, like soft fabric pulled over sunwarmed skin.

The clouds came soon after thick and low, like someone had peeled the roof off a memory and let it float.

And that's when Vihaan felt it.

Not the loneliness.

Not the fear of what was coming.

But the awe of it all.

To be here 35,000 feet in the air with nothing anchoring him but a seatbelt and a lifetime of becoming.

To be this far from the sea,

and still carry its scent in his breath.

He reached into his bag.

Pulled out nothing.

Because he didn't need to hold anything now.

Everything he loved was already in his fingers,

in the curve of his back,

in the silence he now wore like second skin.

He looked out the window again.

The sky was endless.

But not empty.

And in its stillness, he whispered:

"This is not leaving.

This is lifting."

There was no one in the seat next to him.

Just an untouched pillow.

A folded blanket.

A pair of unclaimed headphones resting quietly against the armrest.

But Vihaan could feel her.

Not as an apparition.

Not as an ache.

But as a texture in the air.

Like steam rising from morning tea.

Like the smell of turmeric that lingered hours after the rasam had been cleared.

Aachi hadn't left him.

She had simply changed shape.

He turned slightly, not enough for anyone to notice.

But just enough to say it softly, under his breath:

"You'd have liked this window."

The hum of the aircraft answered like a lullaby.

He closed his eyes for a moment, and there she was not in her sari, not with her garlands or glasses, but in the posture of his spine, the steadiness of his breathing, the way his hands lay open in his lap instead of clenched.

She had taught him that.

Not with instructions.

But with presence.

She had taught him how to wait, how to serve without being seen, how to pray with hands full of rice and still offer everything.

He remembered her voice from years ago, when he asked what grief felt like.

She'd said:

"Like sunlight through a shut window. You feel it. But it doesn't warm the same."

And now, he finally understood.

She wasn't gone.

She had entered him.

Not loudly. Not even fully.

But like salt enters water unseeable, but everywhere.

He looked down at his palms. These were her hands too.

Used for work.

Soft with warmth.

Stained with spice, with ink, with kindness.

He smiled.

And for a moment, Vihaan swore he could feel her not in the chair...

...but in the stillness between his heartbeat and the hum of the world. There's something about flying.

Not the height.

Not the destination.

But the way it stops time.

Mid-air, no clocks matter. No cities pull at your ankles. There's only this space wide, soundless, soft as a held breath where the only thing that moves is memory.

Vihaan leaned his head back and let the silence inside him stretch its limbs.

He didn't think of lectures or blueprints.

He didn't think of job offers or cities left unread in brochures. Instead, his mind walked barefoot through old places.

And in that quiet, he gathered the lessons that never came with titles.

He had learned:

That sometimes, the people who sit at the back of the room are the ones carrying everyone else.

That pain doesn't always cry. Sometimes it brews quietly in the mess hall and waits for someone to pass the curd.

That real love doesn't arrive like a parade. It arrives like folded laundry, shared silence, and a cup of tea poured just right.

That grief isn't a wound to be stitched. It's a window you learn to keep open.

That kindness is a kind of engineering:

It requires design.

It must bear weight.

It must hold others even when you're crumbling inside.

That soft boys grow up to be strong men —

not because they harden,

but because they don't.

Outside the window, the clouds curled like white rivers beneath him. He imagined dropping these lessons like petals into the sky letting them drift downward, landing on balconies, on rooftops, on someone's waiting palm.

He didn't want to write a manifesto.

He just wanted to live gently.

Like Aachi did.

Like Meera did.

Like the world could if only more people remembered how.

He opened his eyes.

The plane hummed.

The world was still far below.

But Vihaan for the first time felt entirely here.

No longer suspended.

Just held.

He glanced at his reflection in the airplane window.

Not sharp, not full just a faint sketch of a man surrounded by sky. A silhouette more than a face.

But it was enough.

Because for the first time, Vihaan saw himself not through what he was planning to do... but through what he had quietly become.

He had not set out to be inspiring.

He had not memorized kindness like a curriculum.

Had not mastered the art of presence like a formula.

But somehow, over time between folding bedsheets and pouring tea, between helping strangers and holding space he had softened into someone the world leaned toward.

Not because he was the loudest.

Not because he had the best words.

But because he listened.

Because he remained.

Because he let people feel safe enough to be unedited around him.

He smiled at the thought.

He had no medals. No framed testimonials. No standing ovations waiting at the arrivals gate.

What he had was weightless and more valuable than anything he could pack in a suitcase.

He carried:

- The scent of jasmine in a foreign sky.
- The rhythm of Aachi's hands, stitched into his decisions.
- The memory of Meera's smile beside waves, tucked beneath his ribcage.
- The laughter of friends who once danced with samosas and slept through alarms and taught him how to stay.

He whispered into the window, not looking at anyone, not expecting an answer:

> " *"I didn't become great.*
> *I became present.*
> *And maybe... that's enough."* "

And in that moment, 35,000 feet above the world that built him,
Vihaan finally saw himself clearly.

Not as someone to be admired.

But as someone to be trusted.

And he knew without applause, without certainty that he was exactly the kind of man he once hoped to become.

Aachi left behind no will.

No heirloom tucked into a locker.

No handwritten recipe book.

No necklace passed down from mother to daughter to grandson.

What she left behind was... him.

Vihaan understood this now somewhere above the ocean, where legacy had no zip code.

She had given him no treasure.

But she had gifted him:

- The courage to sit in silence with someone else's sorrow.
- The discipline to sweep a floor as if it were a kind of prayer.
- The strength to hold his words when others rushed to speak.
- The tenderness to place jasmine in tea, not because it changed the flavor — but because it meant care.

He didn't cry.

He simply turned his palm upward on the armrest and felt the ghost of her hand in his.

Not soft.

Not warm.

But familiar.
She had been the blueprint.
And somehow, he had followed it —
not perfectly,
but with reverence.
He remembered her saying once, while folding his clothes:

*""You don't pass on wealth, kanna.
You pass on ways of holding the world.""*

Now, he held it the way she did.
Not tightly.
Not urgently.
But with open hands.
Ready to give.
Willing to lose.
Always offering.
He looked at the clouds below, stretched like pale rivers across the sky.
And whispered:

*""I didn't inherit your things, Aachi.
I inherited your way of being.""*

And in that quiet moment,
Vihaan became someone else's legacy in the making.
A living echo.
A soft continuation.
A house of memory built from breath, grace, and choice.
If he could speak now
not to himself,
not to Aachi,
but to you
he would not raise his voice.

He would look up from his notebook, lean slightly closer, and say:

> *"You don't have to be loud to be strong.*
>   *You don't have to win to be worthy.*
>   *You don't have to carry everyone to be remembered."*

He would remind you:

That the world needs people who wait their turn at the chai stall.

Who pause to tie a friend's shoelace.

Who pick up the last crumb of a memory and hold it like gold.

He would tell you:

That softness is not weakness.

It is resistance.

It is resilience without spectacle.

He'd say:

> *"The world may never applaud the boy who passes the note,*
>   *or the girl who stays up to listen,*
>   *or the friend who remembers your favorite tea."*

But those people they build the world's emotional infrastructure.

They are the real engineers of humanity.

He'd smile, softly, and close his notebook.

Not because he was done.

But because the sky outside had opened enough to let him begin again.

The seatbelt sign flickered on.

The plane prepared to descend.

And in that moment above a city not yet named,

Vihaan pressed his hand to the window,

and whispered the only thing that ever truly mattered:

> *"I come from people who built love with their hands.*
>   *I leave with nothing.*

And everything.""

The End

9 7 9 8 8 9 9 2 9 0 3 9 8